M000224117

S.G.PUBLISHING

STREET GENERALS III
CAN'T STOP, WON'T STOP

BOOG DENIRO

First print 4/2014

BOOKSTORE DISTRIBUTION
Contact:

www.facebook.com/sgpublishing
www.twitter.com/sgpublishing
sgpublishingllc@gmail.com

Cover design by: Omar Jennett, for S.G. Publishing

Place orders via our e-mail.

Printed in the United States of America

ACKNOWLEDGEMENTS

Just the thought of me doing this shit is still deep for many who know me. I write RESPECT THE STRUGGLE, they hail me one of the realist of this era. I write some thought provoking shit, y'all act like ya boy falling off. I do this shit because I love this shit , because there was a sense that I couldn't do anything else but push hard white. Not just from me, but many who me. I just want to say I appreciate all those who believe in me, those who support me, those who constantly mob with me through *my* struggles.

Y'all know who y'all be. Therefore, I won't be name dropping this go round.

Always us, never them! That's it!

3

This book is dedicated to my biological pops,
John "Pop" Haywood,
of Harlem, USA. Some things are still sacred, Pops.

Previously

In

Street Generals

Capri couldn't remember Action's beloved princess ever looking better. Every tress of her long dark mane was in place. Her eyes were slanted just like Christine's, but shaped like almonds with glowing brown orbs. Her lips were pouty, and her teeth were a thing of perfection – thanks to the work of braces. With the height of her miscreant father, and the beautiful curves of her introverted mother, she was a physically blesses specimen. Round tits, profound hips, and amount of ass. But then again, prior to that sumly afternoon Capri had always viewed her as a sibling, making her off limits to him and anyone he knew. Now, like a luscious piece of forbidden fruit, the five-foot-eight PYT was ripe for the taking. Capri couldn't believe his luck when that white J30 pulled up alongside his 850i at a traffic light on 125th Street. He hit his horn, and they made eye contact. "Pull over right here, Madison Ave, by A Taste of Seafood," he urged forcing a smile.

Grinning and giddy, she said something to her passenger, then veered to her right. Not only did she park up, but she hopped out and ambled over, her passenger not far behind before he was parked.

Zest was in the passenger seat of the 850i, and in a low pitch suggested they bound her pretty little wrists and mouth with duct tape, stick her somewhere safe, send Action a ransom note, and if the demand wasn't met pronto, clip one of those pretty little toes she had peeping out her Prada pumps and leave it at one of Action's establishments. But Capri had grander ideas, something so sinister that even he began to wonder was he losing his mind.

"I see you back in Harlem, huh?" he had sent Katrina's way when she got to his window.

She spoke to Zest first, receiving a head nod from him, then said, "Why shouldn't I be? I'm from Harlem just like you."

"After that incident at the Lux games, your father came

through with the Action pack, and shut the block down. Oh yeah, and he ran up in a crib or two, I believe. You don't think that made some people mad?"

Her body was tightly bound in a sexy black cat suit, and Capri was looking right at the cleft where her legs comlected when she said, "I didn't think he would get that angry when I told him about it. He's usually so kind and sweet. But then again, I am the fruit of his loins. And which one of them bitches giving you face anyway? Christine or Tyam1a?"

"I don't kiss and tell," Capri told her on some real smooth shit, one hand on his crotch, the other on the wheel. And while she was digesting his elusive response, he said, 'Tm shooting out to Miami, 'sup you try'na go do it wild big with me?"

"Wild big?" she grinned.

"I will be twenty-three next week." "For how long?"

"About a week"

"I gotta see if it's okay with my father." "How old are you now? Nineteen?" "Eighteen, going on nineteen."

"You're old enough to be making your own decision now, Trina."

Something about that statement didn't rest well with Katrina. Mainly because she couldn't believe Capri was encouraging her to defy her parents. Yet, she chose to ignore Capri's obvious disregard for Action's authority instead of becoming suspicious. Having enjoyed the fruits of her father's treachery all her life, Katrina pretty much wanted for nothing, and showed her gratitude with obedience and never transgressing. But there was something missing, and that something happened to be relevance some place other than home, somewhere other than with family. And as of lately she'd been having this secret craving for a small morsel of the streets and its many extremities. So it was no surprise to her when she said, "Let me think about it."

Iris said, "What's there to think about?"

2004

CHAPTER ONE

"Dave, I think somebody's following us, were the unwitting words of the driver navigating the dark Lincoln truck, his eyes glued to the rearview mirror.

From his slouching position in the passenger seat, Scarface Dave, an unsavory character, even in his own hood, replied, "Nigga's ain't crazy, bee. Keep driving! That is what I pay you for, right?"

Since the beginning of time, it had always been arrogance propelling bad judgment. It was no different today, especially in the mean streets. Lex, Alexander Merchant, the driver, knew this, yet he complied and veered off at the next exit, his temperature rising by the second. As of late, there had been a rash of shootings and carjackings with no solid motive.

Lex whipped the wheel though. He made a middle class salary driving for fools. $1500 a week which could double if narcotics were in the car. Benefits included free weed and premium liquor. There were risks that came with the gig, like today, but it would take much more to deter him. The money was too good, and so was the association.

As he maneuvered the vee, he recalled the first time driving for his employers. He was only sixteen, a speed demon with an affection for cars. Stolen cars. It was autumn 1996, he didn't recall the exact date, but the summer was over, and everywhere he turned someone had on Avirex leathers and Gortex boots. Anyway, his hood was under siege. As he cozied behind the wheel of a stolen Lex, he could hear all the gun clapping coming off of University Ave. and Feathered Lane, by the housing project raising him. Fearful inhabitants raced to safety as Lex crept to the danger, a war zone. He arrived to witness Lava and Dave taking on a kid with an AK and another dude with some automatic shit. Three had died; the kid with the AK-47, and two boys his age from his projects. The House. Several others were wounded. It was like the scene from the movie Heat, broad daylight shit!

Sitting there amazed, Lex couldn't believe it when the danger came charging toward him. Prior to that day he didn't even know the two murderers knew he existed. More than willing, he assisted, getting them out the area; under major duress. Cops were everywhere, scouring and sweeping the streets for suspects. Even with checkpoints and dragnets, still Lex managed to evade the pursuit. He wasn't impressed with his own deeds, what struck him was that Scarface Dave nor Lava, his right hand man, did any hiding. They were back on the Ave. the very next night, while every DJ and radio personality worth his or her name was sending REST IN PEACE shout outs to the Homie 730. A member of the notorious Murder Gang.

Eight years later, Scarface Dave and Lava were still around, the governing body of Lex's neighborhood, a territory once run by long-dead Tackhead. And he was still their driver, eight years later.

That spring day, the Cross Bronx Expressway was undergoing its usual 4 o'clock rush hour traffic. And the Corvette tailing the SUV couldn't go unnoticed. Scarface Dave peeped the shiny two-door in the mirror on the passenger side of his brand new toy, told his baby faced chauffeur, "Hit a right at the first light on the Castle Hill exit."

The tailing sports car did the same, slowly pulling up as the light on White Plains Road, a main artery in the Bronx infrastructure, turned red.

Scarface Dave reached under his seat for his Glock 27, told his driver, "Next corner, pull over, and leave it in drive."

Dave had the type of reputation goons made livings off of. The kind of rep less fortunate thugs dreamed of achieving. The kind that got the affection of all the hoodrats, got him into the hottest clubs in New York's metropolis without being searched. The kind that got a muthafucka a six foot deep grave, or a five-by-nine cell if one wasn't careful. And over the latter half of the 90s, on into the new millennium, Dave had been beefing up his little resume whenever necessary and with little hesitation.

A busy bodega with a bright red awning that read GROCERY was on the corner, flanked by lots of alert people who could keep a witness box occupied, fingering them it a prosecutor needed it.

Lex noticed that and immediately wished he hadn't left the soft, warm flesh of the thick cutie he'd been spending lots of time with, early this morning. Wished he had ignored Scarface Dave's call.   Made Lex think of the shootout again, then the gun battle at the bottom of Macombs Road that left a well known and feared gangster with a limp. Couldn't forget the fifteen-year-old boy he crushed, not far from where Nitty's body was discovered.

And then the boiler room execution of Bornsavior "Bones" Quinnonez. Regardless of all the treachery and the potential retribution, Dave reveled in his glory. They were the many jewels decorating his reputation.

Lex could feel it, the beginning of the end, did everything he could to avoid Dave's mean eyes as his boss hopped down out the truck with furrowed brows and tight lips. Violence wasn't Lex's thing, which is probably why his unstable hands fidgeted as he tried lighting his cigarette. "Dave what if it's the police?" he stammered, after pulling on his cig.

"Since when police start riding solo in the city, stupido???"

"Right," Lex replied, then under his breath added, "Might not'a been such a bad thing, if it was."

With his weapon tucked near his right hamstring, Dave approached the vehicle tailing him without caution. No one in eye shot could seem to mind their business, having caught a glimpse of the firearm, and Dave didn't care, which made Lex even more uneasy. As he neared the driver's side door, the light tint began to descend giving Dave a clear view of the waiting driver.

"My bad, thought you was somebody else. He got a Navigator just like that one."

It was a woman, one he'd never seen. No malice in her eyes or demeanor. And her voice, it was dripping with the sweetness of a man's favorite confections. Sass!

An uneasiness suddenly overcame Dave, and the girl caught on instantly, which made her nervous for some reason. Slyly, Dave slipped his weapon into the back pocket of his jeans and planted his narrow ass against the Corvette. Not because he didn't want the juicy chick eyeing him to see the gun, but because a cop cruiser was bending the corner, a pair of icy blue eyes with a grueling glare maneuvering the car. The inhabitants of the residential neighborhood knew the pair of officers for their questionable tactics, and ogled more intently to see how things would now unfold. The shiny Corvette and the gleaming Lincoln truck caught the policeman's eye. Just the stare made her even more uncomfortable. But nothing followed. The cop cruiser continued north and she thought it be best she wrap things up.

Lex sparked another Newport and let out a sigh of relief just as Dave said, "You almost got yourself in some trouble, lil mama."

The girl said, "Not by design. And I could say the same thing about you, carrying guns around."

"You saw that, huh?"

"Wasn't I suppose to?"

"Rather be caught with it than without it, ma."

"So you always breaking laws?"

Dave said, "No, I'm always protecting my interests."

'Well, you're not who I was checking for, so I guess I'll be going. I don't want no trouble."

Dave pointed to his truck. "There's not another Navigator on the streets that fuckin' hot." He was feeling himself, with both hands, figuratively speaking of course. "So I don't know how you got us mixed up, but it's your story so I'ma let you tell it. Go ahead."

"Only things I see different is the rims."

"Twenty-trays, babe!" he boomed, then directed her to his sound system which Lex was now blasting. "You hear that? Five grand in music. Nothing but the best, babe!"

She smirked thinking of this other cat he reminded her of.

Young cat going by Five who was a fiend for attention, always causing attraction, and tried extra hard to be noticed by her. He was arrogant just like Dave, so full of himself, and not so good looking either. The only thing she found remotely interesting about Five was that a year ago no one had even knew who he was, almost like he'd come up overnight. But that wasn't important at the moment, getting in good with Dave was. He had what she wanted.

"Okay, well it was nice meeting you," she spat, smiling at Dave in a way he could easily find to be flirtatious.

"You're coming onto me right? Want me to ask you for your number and all that, huh?" he sounded off, the sunlight bringing attention to his choppy teeth, which also reflected an enamel deficiency. "Your tactics, I think it's interesting, sexy too I must admit."

She laughed lightly, her boobs bouncing purposefully.

"But I'm not going to ask, you're gonna ask for my number," he added.

"And why would I do that? I've never asked a dude for his number. I will ask where you are from though?"

"Right here in the Bronx. And you, where you from?"

"Queens, but I've been living uptown for a long time now. And you, I thought you were a Bronx dude."

"How?"

"I can tell. Real cocky, like Bronx niggahs," she told him while checking his style. He was dressed like a winner. But no fault of his, he just didn't have those features that would make a woman want to touch his face, or feel as though her soul was lit on fire, looks that would create immediate sexual tension. Even before he was scarred for life, ripped with a razor across the face,

14

the mirror just wasn't something he paid close attention to. He was tall with lanky arms just like his gangly mother, and had gnome-like features he got from his pops. But those faces of death garnishing America's currency never ceases to elevate a man's confidence. If Flava Flav could find love, why couldn't Scarface Dave?

Prior to his change of fortune, Dave was just another insignificant, bottom-feeding, non-descript felon dwelling in the wells of society. He was putting holes in targeted individuals for petty cash, killings that wouldn't even produce lawyer money if prosecuted. He was fooling with females no true player would even entertain. All while holding residence on his mother's love seat in the Sedgwick Houses which he had to beat several felines to. And now he had the attention of women who could make money off their appeal, and no longer carried the scent of cat litter. No more chipping in for cheap weed, sharing 40 ounce beers, or eliciting the affection of rundown slut buckets. He now had a name substantiated by relevance, that was synonymous with rival gang leaders. Despair and desperation, hunger and harassment had been banished and replaced by an air of entitlement, and it showed when he said, "I'm taking you out tonight."

The girl said, "And how you plan on doing that if you don't ask for my number?"

Dave was confident he would have his way with her. One could accredit that to the greed within. Or, he like most men, wanting everything in his path. Unable to avoid loving with the eyes. A common defect most successful men suffer from.

"I said I'm taking you out, now gimme your number."

She released this sensuous sigh that made her breasts rise and settle, and Dave's beady eyes become unapologetic. His orbs were now all over her. Her bosom, her thighs, toes and eyes. She was smooth, like the cool breeze drifting up Castle Hill Avenue. Dave began to think about his dark skin all over her vanilla body, them being so close he wouldn't be able to tell where she began or where he ended. Men with concubines weren't suppose to be having thoughts like that.   But this chick had that star power, and she knew it. It made her somewhat aroused. Her nipples were now hard and erect, penetrating the thin white top she wore with no brassier beneath. Dave took notice and grinned, as her rich dark nipples, clearly visible, made his mouth water.

"You think I'm easy, don't you?" she asked, before flipping her hair back over her shoulder.

"Did I say that? I didn't say that," he stammered, again standing before her with his back to the street and passing cars.

"But your eyes did," she toyed.

"I can't help it; you're bad," he admitted, nodding.

"I would, if there wasn't someone in my life," she said, shifting into an upright posture that made her torso look longer and her camel-toe visible.

"We just hanging out," he shot back quickly.

"I know, but I have rules. One at a time."

Dave thought about her being from Queens, and figured she was on those suburban chicks, a trust fund baby, super ethical, with excessive parental control early on. To some degree, Dave was right. The 26-year-old making him anxious and horny was the product of two conservatives, hard working folks, just as passionate about their country as they were about their pension plans and 401Ks. They were democrats who attended conventions. And they loved their daughter dearly, and had been

16

praying for her more now than ever.

It was as if she could read his mind, and an exultant smile took form of her pouty mouth as she said "I won't give you my number, but I will take your's."

Dave took the pen she gave him, scribbled it on the post-it she too offered, then asked, as he handed her things back, "Who's gonna be calling?"

"How rude of me, Dave," she cooed, "it's Iris..."

$$\$\,\$\,\$$$

There were thousands of Iris' in Queens, and tens of thousands in New York City. But there was no sign of the Iris on Myspace, or any of the dating sites and chat rooms Dave frequented. He had a still image of Iris in his mind, and everywhere he looked he saw her. Still, he was unclear about her ethnicity. Latina?, he wondered. She did have the twang. But her demeanor mirrored one of those strong willed sistahs; like she'd seen a lot with those eyes. The looks though, definitely exotic. Skin tone, texture of hair, body structure, the angle and color of her eyes. And her lips, full and succulent.   Dave   had   been thinking about Iris since she left his sight, anticipating her call, and logging countless hours trying to locate her online.

In a haste, he shut his laptop and shot up to the rooftop where he could take in his entire neighborhood. The view was beautiful. Yankee Stadium, the George Washington Bridge, the close proximity of the East River which added much mystique as it was an alleged dumping ground for making people disappear.

It was never his dream to rule the world, he just wanted a piece. With that came peace of mind, and along the way several pieces of ass.

Dave was on the verge of being thirty, and the thing he feared more than dying in prison was not being taken seriously. It had been years since he faced any real dangers, or threw rocks at a prison. Lava, a man he'd killed with, had took on a sophisticated woman as his girl, one that made a brother want to do right. Dave secretly wondered could the girl he'd just met do that for him?

After 20 minutes of taking in the scenic view from the rooftop of his towering building, he took the stairs, two at a time, back down to the eighth floor where his decked out flat in the PJ's awaited him.

Inside, he leaned back in his Lay-Z-Boy and logged back onto the Internet, thinking Iris would eventually pop up. While surfing the net, in swayed his concubine, posting up barefoot on Dave's alpaca rug. Her toes were done French, as were her fingernails. This one, Dave had paid handsomely for. Not the rug, the pig eon toed babe he first seen in the eye candy section of a rap magazine, before finding out that she did music videos and could be seen up close at a local strip club called "Bada Bing." Turned out she was the Super Head of the Bronx, but Dave could never get tired of looking at her gyrate and writhe to any beat while blowing bubbles. No man could. She loved to chew gum while performing. It had been one of the things that attracted her first two regulars, two taxpaying cats, who came through just for her.

Her breasts were full of joy with honey gold nipples. Her ass wasn't huge, but pleasantly plump, and she had a flat stomach, no muffin top, with hips and thighs tapering right into her small waistline. Just five and a half feet, and 23-years old, her physical features were perfectly proportioned without any of the surgical enhancements dancers had began turning to for bigger profits.

18

She patronized the city in expensive red sewn-in weaves just a little darker than her own henna hue which probably had something to do with her name being Scarlet the Red Bone.

One night while straddling Dave, a new regular she thought resembled Omar from the "Wire", she told him she was in the midst of some serious decision making. That she had considered giving up the pole, print modeling in scanty clothing, and video cameras, for something much more lucrative. And that if she took it she'd be moving to Atlanta.

"What?" he quizzed caressing her backside softly.

"It includes branding and merchandise," she simpered, popping her gum at the same time.

"What?" he poked, and she whispered it in his ear.

Dave said, "Fuck that, come home with me, be my personal porn star. I got money."

Her response had been, "I know you have money, but the deal is worth five figures, a high five."

"How many dudes coming in here trying to whisk you away to anywhere your heart desires?"

Zero! And neither was he, but it was close.

Scarlet could have become the Jenna Jamison of urban porn had Dave not beat Zest to the club that night.

She was thankful Dave had talked her out of porn, thankful he'd taken her in and listened to a heart that had been broken so many times she wasn't sure it would ever play another love song. Scarlet didn't love Dave though. But in the nine months of sharing time and space with him, strong feelings had developed. But she needed more, and the last few days it was feeling more like they were digressing instead of moving towards that place called love. And at 24 now, with more and more youngsters jumping the broom, Scarlet was beginning to have thoughts of more.

"You been on that computer for the last week, babe. What's up?

"And--?"

Scarlet said, "Look at me."

"I see you?"

"If you don't want to see me, I'm going to the club," she threatened, her provocative eyes cutting like claws.

"You wanna go to the club, go ahead! Just make sure you beat me home!"

Scarlet was startled. He never wanted her to go to the club.

"Are you serious?"

After appraising his own words briefly, he said, "Hell no! But can't you see I'm, busy?" She turned on some music.

Her very first Club Mom at her very first strip joint, a lady from Harlem named Maliah, who'd also helped her through a hard time or two, once said, "Love is like magic, a whole bunch of illusions. So just focus on the fun, and maybe you'll create magic... but if you don't, at least ya had fun."

Scarlet was wearing boyshorts only, red lace, so tight her camel toe showed.   She was now a few inches from Dave's face, and she was ready for some fun. Made Dave think of Iris again. A sophisticated sistah?

Scarlet went to his soft spot.

Dave could feel her tongue on his lobe as she perched herself on the arm of his chair. Then her hand beneath his laptop, caressing his member. That was it for the online search. Dave's face went left running right into Scarlet's sweet mouth. Kissing her deeply and fondling her a bit, she used her attentive hands to bring him to erection. Soon he would be penetrating her pretty little gash, and remembering he didn't need another chick. Just as he leaned the Lay-Z-Boy back, the screen on his phone lit up.

Everything stopped.

Both their eyes were on his Sidekick. He reached!

But she beat him to it.

"Hello!"

"Can ... I speak t o Dave?"

"Here! I knew it! I could feel the shit!" sulked Scarlet as she tossed the phone at Dave with some serious speed on it.

Dave already knew who it was.

CHAPTER TWO

The jail shit was really beginning to get to Christine. Every time she turned around it was something discouraging her loyalty. If her dude wasn't in the box, he was lacking in the emotional support department. It was driving her crazy to say the least. No question, he was worth all the changes, all the challenges, but eight years of the shit was enough to make any woman cry. He was only suppose to be doing five years -- four years and two months with good time. She'd counted it to the day, monitoring a calendar each and every year that passed. And he could have, if he didn't always have something to prove.

One thing she couldn't deny, he'd always been that way, for as long as she'd known him, and of him. Down right stubborn. To his credit though, he made sure she was well off before he went away.

The only thing missing? The ring on the fourth finger of her left hand, and the accompanying commitment to love and cherrish her.

That would've been nice. That would've meant conjegal visits, keeping their passion feverish. She deserved it, didn't she?

Every time she looked at their vastly growing child, who resembled him so much, she would rewind back to the days of their sordid beginnings, the unplanned affair, when he'd highlight her life in ways she didn't think was possible.

She was a love child, their baby girl, conceived on Christine's eighteenth birthday, in the back row of a dark movie theater on 16lst Street. Back in those days he could have Christine wherever he wanted, any way he liked. And he had a main girl she was very much aware of. Said a lot about him.

Four or five years her senior, he was far more advanced than she, with the exception of sexuality, which is where her advantage lied. With a gansta aura as grand as his, that came as a surprise. But something she relished. He had all the connections, all the answers, and all the things she found attractive in a man. The tattoos, the muscles, even the buck-fifty on his cheek.

Through it all, which wasn't long, a few months at most, she'd been accused of setting his girl up to be kidnapped -- something she was quickly cleared of. Even played a major role in him solving his mother's murder. Did it knowing he would take matters into his own hands, exacting revenge in the worse way. There were days that bothered her, how he doubted her respect, and how he used her fascination with him to his advantage.

In the end, she got him, the money, and she had his first child. But she also lost a lot. There wasn't a dude on that gansta shit willing to entertain her; and if a regular nigga did find interest, just for some small talk, possibly a good time her daughter would chase them off.

She was lonely. Very!

Her best friend Tyanna was dead, her estranged father Act ion was dead, her half-sister Katrina, a memory -- all gunned down the dame night, in a two block radius. Oh, and a federal agent, who just happened to be the father of her man's ex-girlfriend. Though she didn't have a relationship with her pops or her sis, and she and Tyanna were on bad terms at the time of her departure, it always seemed to take up residence in her conscience.   Their violent fates, and the inescapable reality that she may have the answers to some very important questions the FBI would love to have. That wasn't easy living with, even if the suspicions were wrong.

Just as she was finishing off a chilled glass of Moscato, she was having with chocolate covered strawberries, the telephone rang. And for some reason the sound was rather arousing. Toys just didn't do it for her anymore. Not the Rabbit, nor the Bullet, or the warm pulsating water sprouting from her shower head. She squeezed her legs together tightly, then answered the phone, thinking: I need the attention of a man.

"Collect call from -- Capri!"

She heard the procedures so many times that she cut the chase and pressed the button, "Your call has been accepted."

"What's really good, yo?"

That's how things were. No pleasantries.

Before saying a word, Christine reached for her treasure chest and located the hidden jewel that held the ability to make her whole body glisten with ecstasy. Upon making contact with her clitoris, she used the sound of him breathing, and the ruggedness of his voice to add to the pleasure she was suddenly feeling.The two closest fingers to her right thumb became moist from the warmth of her insides. Oh what a feeling, she thought, this lovely smirk slowly overwhelming her face.

"Christine, what up???"

"Hey, how are you?" she moaned, rather indulgingly.

"I'm aiight."

Christine was almost there, where she needed to be. Her hand had become a savior of some sort. And there seemed to be nothing to complain about. Every woman needed that feeling. And she wasn't the exception. She was a very attractive girl.

Shapely, with a cocoa brown hue, long raven hair, cover girl facial features, and a cleanliness that even God would be impressed with. Even after giving birth to a seven pound baby she carried the full term, her body took no hits, returning right back to its richness and even better in six weeks. She couldn't go anywhere without turning heads, or provoking compliments. In six waves, she had released lots of tension, exhaling as she purred, "I'm all right too."

"What's up with my daughter?"

"Just did her hair earlier."

"What about you, how you got your hair?"

Christine wiped her hand on her skirt, deciding she'd shower and change, then said, "Wash and set, Chinese bang, nothing major."

"You still polishing my daughter's nails?"

"She cries if I don't," Christine informed Capri, heading for her bedroom with her glass and bottle in tow. "When are you coming home? This house feels emptier and emptier with each day you're there."

"Soon. What up with Zest and Stink?"

"I hardly see Zest anymore. And Stink, he's doing him." As Capri countered, Christine couldn't help but think:

Everybody's grown up, but you. He was even more deep into the gang life these days than ever before, and very high in the ranks. He loved his set and his homies with just as an intense passion as he did the family he had waiting for him to return empathy! The space that has come between us is just increasing!"

Stink could hear the discern in her voice. The funny thing though, he was well aware of her unhappiness and the reckless decisions the troubles fostered. But quite frankly, he was in no position to be pointing out transgressions. All he could do was hope for the best, and anticipate the worse. Capri was a seasoned criminal with psychopathic behavior. Bottom line! Christine just didn't want to accept that reality when everyone else had long ago.

"When did he get the parole hit?"

"A year and some change ago," Christine remembered.

"How much change?"

Christine thought for a minute, said, "About seven months."

A year and seven months ago.   I remember it like it was yesterday..."

Stink too remembered.

CHAPTER THREE

It was a balmy evening in the Bronx. Didn't have the romantic flow of Rome at night, but the stars were shining down, the skies were clear and the moon was full. Iris left her Riverside Drive apartment loudly singing the words to Mary J. Blige's very first hit, Real Love: "I'm searching for a real love! Real love! I'm searching for a real love!" She knew the words by heart, as was the case with most of her favorite tunes. Music was the sound track to her life. And she needed to be in a good mood that night.

They'd almost missed each other. Dave was on a different set of wheels, and Iris was on heels. Both were dressed comfortably he in tan linen, and she in a sexy cocktail dress and studded open toes. Big designer shades covered her eyes when Dave finally realized he had driven right by her twice. Iris's lower back did one of the best dips he'd ever seen. The way it rolled right into her butt and made her hips jut forward. He'd never seen anything sexier. And anyone looking could tell she'd left her panties and bra home.

He pulled up and said, "Where's the Vette?"

"Belongs to a friend. No parking in the city, so I don't have a car."

Scarface Dave looked around then hopped out and opened

"It is what it is," she shot back raising her right hand.

Dave just stared, then said, "So you like to powder your nose?"

"Makes me do crazy things," she said, just before the pure white vacuumed up one nostril, and then next. She had this cute little micro spoon that slid right back into this little tiny silver tube that held approximately three and a half grams.

Her mind traveled to her one and only true love, the man who had introduced her to the insidious drug. She recalled sniffing it right off of him, and the ecstasy that followed before he was jailed.

She looked over at Dave and thought, the cut running across the center of his face and down towards his right jaw line is rather impressive. Wonder who did it?

He, on the other hand, was having second thoughts. Iris was definitely appealing, super bad, but this wasn't a problem he wanted. Scarlet was hassle enough -- the stripping, male friends, the nude photos online -- but her only addictions were bucks and dick. He killed the engine and said, "Come on, yo!"

Casa Marie's was a four star restaurant with an array of bilingual chefs, mostly from the west coast, each seasoned in their very own cuisine. The bar was stocked with premium liquors and wines with the best cocktail waitresses serving it up.

Since its opening only six months ago it was always packed and never failed to impress. The decor made patrons feel like they'd left the city and entered some quaint fixture in Costa Rica. The owner was usually there to greet visitors at the door; and this day was no different. She wasn't the prettiest woman, but she had her moments. Many! And like today, in the right light and the right outfit, she was visually interesting.

Iris saw her approaching, cheeks flush like she'd just been blushing, and immediately thought she has a lot to be happy about.

And then their cheeks met.

"Hi, mami," they both said at the very same time. While giving Iris the onceover, she also took a peek at Dave. "You look adorable, Iris."

"Thank you," Iris said, the blast she'd just shoveled up her nose just taking its affect.

They were quickly seated in an area where water was immediately brought. But before Iris could get comfy and entertain anymore of Dave's questions, she noticed another familiar face. "Wildlife!" she called.

"Where you think you're going?" Dave wanted to know, disapproving all the fraternizing. But Iris continued on with her sexy stroll, generating stares.

"Wildlife!"

A smooth fella turned back and pretended to be surprised as though he hadn't seen her enter. "Oh shit, what's popping, sis?"

"Let's just say -- I'm not myself tonight. What up with you?"

"Came through for a quick bite."

"By yourself?"

Wildlife stuck his hands in the pockets of his cargos, said, "By myself."

"You never go nowhere without though. What's poppin?"

"By myself," he repeated and stared towards the front door. "You already know what pop. Get money, stay fly, pop heat! We do it all."

Iris couldn't quite put her finger on it, but something wasn't right. Wildlife brought his eyes back to her just as she took her shades off. "You know my nigga be home in about a month, right?"

"That's what's poppin'. He deserve it."

Iris nodded thinking of how much Wildlife had come up.

He was one of the big boys, done big things. Nice jewels, nice cars, nice taste in women, and he was a nice looking dude. So she couldn't help but wonder why he didn't have one of his many conquest at his hip. But she thought better to let him get going so she could get back to Dave glaring at her from across the restaurant.

"When was the last time you spoke to Zest?"

Wildlife said, "Been a minute. I spoke to him not too long ago. "

"You know he gonna want to get the whole crew back together."

"Same blood type, can't stop won't stop! So you already know I'm there.

"You got my number, right?"

"Yup," she said putting her frames back on.

"Who that?" Wildlife asked too noticing the grimace on Dave's face.

"All I'm say right now, Iris get 'em -- Iris got 'em," Iris said.

Iris was back at her seat and smiling before Wildlife had finally realized what she was alluding to. Not the part about Capri's homecoming, but the part about the cat sitting across from her. Not many knew she was vicious as a viper, very deliberate and so efficient, or that a lot of the work that was being put in was her work. She was not more than 5'5" on heels, a hundred and twenty pounds, and one of the city's best kept secrets when it came to the murder game.

As Wildlife sidled up to the edge of the window where he could peek in without being noticed by the patrons, he suddenly realized who the dude sitting across from Iris was. She's good, Wildlife thought as he watched her entangle this kid in her coils. Smiling and shit! Touching and all that. He could only wonder what they had in store for the violator? And why not just leave his ass dead in the streets? Then he felt his blood began to boil. Was it retribution for young BB's chest being collapsed beneath the wheels of the hijacked vehicle Iris's acquaintance used to escape death? Or was it revenge for the limp he gave Stink? Or, the kidnapping and murder Bones suffered at the hands of that niggah?

Wildlife began to run his hand over his baby face, his eyes narrowing in disgust. Though he had been distant from his immediate circle over the last year, nothing could pierce through the love he had for them.

The owner neared the hostess's podium, and Wildlife's orbs left Iris and followed her every step. Cars were speeding by behind him, horns were blaring, music polluted the streets, yet his focus was razor sharp. The owner moved so gracefully, and the wedding band adorning her hand spoke volumes. She was important. Her ambiance screamed it!

For some reason, even as he stared intently, Zest came to mind. He was certainly doing his own thing too. When Zest told him what he was planning the last time they spoke, Wildlife couldn't believe it. That was just a month ago. The run Wildlife had with Zest as his connect was one of legend. They really had it for cheap, and Wildlife was able to live out one of his many dreams! So when he heard Zest say he'd run through all his spoils, it was like hearing the Towers had fallen all over again. Tragic. He estimated him to be worth at least ten mill in 2001, twice as much in 2002. Zest was the go-to man like the leading rusher in a tight football game in January. Always reliable.

Wildlife got back to the clear and present -- Casa Marie.

CHAPTER FOUR

Directly outside of Harlem Auto Sound, a trendy new establishment in the heart of upper Manhattan where everyone from celebs to street dons brought their cars to have the sound systems customized, something big was going down. Photogs, reporters, and all sorts of other press people were teeming like the jackels they were. Donned in a track jacket he wore open, matching kicks, a bright white T beneath and blue jeans, the proud owner stood poised and prepared to take the next step in his journey.

He had always been about changing the conditions of his people. But it wasn't until the Towers were toppled that his awareness really began to propel. To see such a diverse city in all its division come together was inspiring. One summer evening as he was making his exodus from the Kingdome, a basketball tournament sponsored by Dame Dash, a sad story had fallen on his ears. He happened to be with a couple of his comrades who were more interested in getting out of there safely than what the frail woman was complaining about.

The woman happened to be requesting donations from all the hustlers in an attempt to get her seventeen-year old son a good lawyer. He'd been accused of a double murder Stink knew for sure the boy had not committed.

The very next day he had enough money dropped off with the woman to retain private counsel and a private investigator. A month later he got with a friend of his and began a series of conferences with a couple of law students and activist. A plan was devised that all included parties believed could make a difference. It wouldn't be as powerful as the movement Russel Simmons and Jay-Z was working on, the abolishing of the Rockerfeller Law, but it would be as appreciated, and his contribution to the fixing of a system that was enslaving his community at rapid proportions.

He'd wanted to assemble a cast of competent advocates like the renown defense counsel William Counsil to come in and teach the youth the law, inform them of their Constitutional rights, while also aiding the wrongfully accused and convicted in their guest for vindication. Reduced sentences was one thing, but sentences where there shouldn't be was another.

As one law student had said -- "Prosecutors should not be on a sole guest for convictions, but a guest to seek truth whether it leads to a conviction or not!" This girl was a pretty twenty-three year old studying criminal justice at NYU. Pretty in the way movie stars were. When Stink had smiled at her that day, from across the huge conference table she amended that truth with: "Trial is not a mere sporting event, but a necessary process in our justice system."

And what better way for Stink to give back to a gang ridden community, where entire generations of men were being removed and were serving lengthy prison terms?

Now that he no longer sported the gold grilled smirk and the cornrows, Stink would easily pass for the actor Morris Chestnut.

But, it would take more than a makeover, losing his

penchant for the gang culture, and a little community service to convince the media that he was a changed man.

The whole scene was unreal, unfamiliar and otherworldly. The people, the cameras, the press. There was no podium, no script, and the only thing that mattered was the pandemonium. It was the biggest day of Stink's life, the most meaningful. Bigger than the day he took his oath, the day he took his vows. Bigger than the grand opening of Harlem Auto Sounds. And all were extremely significant pieces to his puzzle.

There were hundreds of eyes on him, mostly the eyes of a historically deprived race, eager for change. Some he knew, but most he didn't. What did it matter? They were all there for the same cause.

Not far away, but well nestled, was his muscle. A burly light skinned fellow in his late twenties, and two short stocky brothers who appeared much older than they really were. The trio wasn't the usual suspects Stink rolled with. They were bouncers with military backgrounds he used from time to time at his gambling spot which was more like an underground casino. Only his showgirls were nude, and there was an invitation only policy.

"Word is you're running around town masquerading as an activist, but you're really heavily entrenched in a gang!" jabbed a slender and sleek European chick with a heavily made up face.

"Mr. Pierce --! Is it true that you were spotted leaving Bada Bing earlier this week with a chart topping rapper who openly admits and continuously pledges his alliance to a gang in his lyrics?" a busty blogger quizzed from a short distance.

"Marcel Pierce, what do you expect to come out of this nonprofit organization you're launching?! Get out of jail free cards for your criminal friends?" bristled a reporter in a cheap suit representing the New York Post.

Stink was stumped, short winded, ready to spaz. That wasn't exactly how he'd expected things to go when he announced the time and date for the launch of his nonprofit organization on his website. He briefly wondered about wifey and why she wasn't there showing her support! Something he rarely did these days; have thoughts of the misses. And then he cursed the woman he was paying handsomely to do his public relations work.

Stink shot back: "Not everyone with dreams are criminals. Not everyone who gets arrested is guilty. Not everyone who breaks the law deserves banishment. And those deserving of punishment should be protected from the prosecutors unwilling to climb upon the shoulders of known falsities, ignoring the truth! It's bad enough that felons are looked upon as second class citizens! That they become part of an abandoned caste. That's what my nonprofit organization is all about! Lawyers being effective."

An array of hand clapping and harmonious clamoring followed those powerful words. The sun seemed a little brighter, shining down on a rising star. Even felt like traffic had subsided on Lenox Ave, tuning into the growing crowd. Stink moved his head in small circles, loosening his neck, while thinking he'd taken their best shot.

Little did he know!

"Word around town is the food's delicious at your wife Rosa Pierce's new Latin restaurant, Casa Marie on the Grand Concourse!" said a vanilla coated female with a supple figure, her Latin accent just as thick as Stink's wife Rosa Marie. "If only the prices could be more affordable... less people committing crimes to have a plate there, maybe."

As Stink prepared to send verbal shells back at her, he was hit with: "Who was the mysterious woman you were photo'd with late two nights ago exiting Megu?"

The inquiry that ached the most had come from a specimen with a sizzling body and a smirk he couldn't quite put his finger on. His mind traveled back five summers ago, the star studded wedding ceremony that literally plunged the couple right onto Hip Hop's social scene of New York City.

Fast forward back to the future -- he was now being challenged on indiscretions, not just affiliations or his checkered past. Something he hadn't planned for. No longer was the underworld his only playground. No longer could he slap the faces of nosy, disrespectful people without suffering consequence. The tables had rotated. He was now fodder. Food for the animals constantly taking chunks out of him every chance they could get. He'd made it all possible, just as he'd made for the exciting life he was now leading.

Stink thought back to the statement he'd made in a 2002 interview to a street savvy reporter working on a documentary about New York's street moguls and their humble beginnings that went something like this"

"In the 90s everyone was breaking the law. Everyone was seeking fame and fortune, taking chances to improve their conditions, to erase that sense of hopelessness, and desperation. Crime was almost celebrated. It was the tail end of Reaganomics! And I was right there."

And it helped none that a few months after the documentary's release, a photo taken in a state penitentiary visiting room of him with convicted killer Capri Hayward managed to surface in a issue of The Street Bible. Nor did it help his image that his father's conviction had been suddenly overturned after seventeen years, and that he was out on appeal bona. Or that he had befriended a city councilman with questionable ethics. Result? The loss of his privacy.

Composed, but still not in charge, Stink shared stares with the eyes in the crowd, prepared to face the accusation when he heard, "Since when has it become a crime in the western world for a married man to share a meal with women other than his wife?!"

The deep, sappy voice belonged to Stink's publicist, a feisty chick with a slick mouth and whip responses. For the last twelve months it had been her responsibility to soften the perception mainstream New York was getting of this goon turned success. In her field, perception was everything. And she genuinely loved her job. It had been Shandy Walton's most exciting assignment to date. She had a sun kissed glow that commanded attention, facial features of an exotic feline, and just enough curves to jam traffic if she desired to. She was well put together. She was charming and generous, not to mention effective in her field.

Since she didn't have children, a lot of her earnings went to Neiman Marcus, Bloomingdales, Sax Fifth, Victoria's Secret, the Fur Factory, and places of the such.

Upon meeting Stink, of course after many unanswered request, she immediately thought nothing about him implied over-aggression. Instead, she noticed something different, an assured confidence that made aggression unnecessary, and also demanded respect. She was also surprised he didn't have a bunch of baby mamas, as good as he looked, and accomplished as he was. She had friends looking to trap men like him. Women with degrees, and careers of their own.

"So why me?" she ribbed, having arrived at Starbucks on

125th Street two minutes after he did the first time they decided to meet.

"You know why," Stink had replied, not knowing what to make of her. She was responsible for making a couple of his chums in the industry not just tolerable, but likeable.

While he was checking her out, Shandy said, "I'll do it!"

"Take me on as a client?"

"Yes!" She seemed excited.

"Fuck me if I don't fall over myself thanking you," Stink poked.

"And that means exactly what, Marcel Pierce?" she wanted to know, her own interpretation splayed across her face.

."You know, forgive me," he answered smiling.

"That's what I thought!" Shandy poked back, stretching out her arm and connecting with Stink's right shoulder.

And with that, her responsibilities began.

Now she was his media maven, and the crowd seemed to simmer. A combination of two things. Her appearance, and her verbal prowess. She glanced over at her client who seemed not to be himself, but somewhat relieved. She'd been watching for several minutes before announcing her presence. She thought the Gucci colors he was wearing looked gorgeous against his dark skin. And couldn't help smiling deep within as the sunrays made the deep waves in his hair spin, having suggested he get rid of the braids and gold grill.

"You're right, it's not a crime in America! So why duck behind the huge pocketbook to avoid the photogs???"

Shandy said, "Because I needed proof that you people would make this about my client's personal life rather than what this is really about!"

"And that is?!" the N. Y. Post guy quipped.

"Accountability Where it counts!" boomed Shandy with pride. "My client's nonprofit organization!"

"So it was you?" the beautiful Latina asked with very little belief written all over her face.

Shandy looked at Stink, he looked at her, and immediately she knew she'd be taking the rest of the day off. "Yesss, we had a great time too. But the food's better at his wife's restaurant!"

Shandy had gotten things under control, then Stink, back to his normal self, got down to business. He took questions, responding smoothly, then ending with, "I chose William Counsil as the mode because I like the way he handled the Larry Davis case, and the way he fought for the kid in the Central Park jogger case.   This city needs more attorney's like him."

"The Central Park Jogger perps confessed! And Larry Davis was a terrorist!"

Stink said, "The jury seemed to think it was self-defense. And the kids in the Central Park Jogger case were badgered into confessions!"

He thanked everyone for coming out, told them he was anticipating their help in this attempt to change things. He noticed a few faces from his Accountability Committee and sent them one of those presidential waves, as well as a charming wink.

The twenty-three old NYU student winked back

CHAPTER FIVE

The Muse Hotel, Downtown, New York. One at a time they entered. The executive suite was registered to a city councilman. As soon as they were enveloped in the cloak of privacy, and their midday interlude had concluded, Shandy said, "Who was the girl you were photo'd with the other night?"

With that arrogant half smile of his -- the one that turned his publicist into his secret lover Stink said, "I'm most definitely appreciative for your quick thinking, that's what I pay you for, but I don't appreciate you questioning me."

"A picture is with a thousand words. Public-relations primer for what a man on the rise shouldn't be doing."

Stink sat up, rolled out of bed and perched himself at the edge of the bed. "Every once in a while a niggah be needing reassurance."

"What do you mean?" Shandy quizzed scooting up to the edge of the bed by Stink.

"Of who I be," he said after a brief delay.

Shandy's slanted eyes located two holes in Stink's right leg the size of fifty cent pieces. Bullet wounds, his battle scars. "How many of us are there?" she quipped pushing her hands back through her lustrous mane. "How many?"

Many!

But when Stink cheated, most of the time he'd just get his thrill off. He didn't date. No meeting up for meals, no meeting of the minds, no confiding in one another about their respected lives; that kind of interaction made things personal and intimate. Almost like kissing. It wasn't something the women liked -- but knowing well received performances usually were followed up with encores, just made them go harder. That's how girlie from two nights ago became an overnight celeb. And, Shandy worthy of an honest answer.

"Before I got shot up, left with this limp, I never cheated on my wife. Shit, my first days of recovery she took me out to Jamaica, had me on a nudist beach and resort. Seeing all those beautiful women... asshole naked."

"And you started cheating there?" Shandy sulked.

"Nah," Stink said remembering the beginning of his disloyalty. The very first time he stepped out on his wife. "Ball was my release. Whenever I felt like wifey wasn't enough, I'd go play basketball. Then my leg -- couldn't play no more."

Shandy rubbed his back, said, "Go on."

"I started going to the games. Courtside seats at the Garden. Started meeting cheerleaders. Met one for the Sixers. Sophisticated sistah like you. Nowhere near as nasty as you though."

Shandy went from his consoler to shooting a right hand. "Shut up!" Her bare breasts, just the right size and shape for her body, heaved with the motion and range of her playful and harmless gesture. "I'm not freaky, unless I'm really into you."

Stink laughed a little, then continued. "The Knicks were playing Philly when I met this cheerleader while exchanging contacts with Allen Iverson. She had a nice smile, dope body, and I ended up on the interstate the very next day. We went to TGI got a room, then we fucked, and fucked. And, I felt no remorse. It was months before I cheated again."

"But you did."

"Yeah."

"Was it the secret life, or the secret desires themselves that made you cheat again?"

"Both!" he turned to her and said. "Being able to keep that shit private; and then feeding my ego in other cities. First it was Philly, then D.C., Miami, Houston and Los Angeles."

"All cheerleaders?"

"I went from cheerleaders to singers, and then dancers."

"Which is why you eventually opened up your gentleman's club?"

"You're not just gorgeous and freaky, you're smart too," Stink whispered against her ear.

Shandy loved his compliments even if they weren't original, and filled with satire. She scooted back a little, almost to the middle of the bed and leaned back on her elbows. He loved her like that. When he didn't have to fantasize about what lied beneath her designer threads. Her legs were splayed just a bit, just enough that if Stink wanted to, he could see her clean shaven vagina.

"Tell me more," she beckoned, unabashed.

Stink stood up, naked as a newborn. "How about I take you on another rough ride before we part ways? How about that?" he shot back pulling her to him. At almost six feet tall he towered over Shandy's petiteness.

"And then you'll tell me more?"

"Maybe," he said fondling her.

It was every women's nirvana, no matter how short a time, to own a man's complete attention. And at that very moment she had Stink's. A man had never paid such close attention to her body as he did. At 29, which wasn't much mileage at all, she had no recollection of her breasts being sucked so sensuously. Her nipples were engorged with passion as was his penis. The pleasure made the suite feel like a palace. She bit down on her bottom lip as he lifted her up and brought her down on his waiting member. He went deep, so deep she could feel him in her soul.   She crossed her ankles behind his back just as he grabbed hold of her butt cheeks, and they bucked at each other like life depended on it. Up and down, up down! And then he slipped out of her, but could still feel her warmth and wetness on the base of his dick.

"Put it back inside me," she purred, beaming with her lips on his.

In that position and many others they spent a little more of the afternoon creating memories. They talked a little more about his needs and desires, her ideas and concerns, and then his phone chirped. While he spoke, she bathed then eased back into her sliver of a thong thinking of the strong sexual connection between them, and how it has got so far in such short time.

Her thoughts sped back to a winter afternoon. He had a two o'clock appointment in which she was briefing him on a few things she has set up for him. Radio, and interviews with two different mags. On his way out he had turned back and kissed her. Caught her by surprise. That kiss led to grasping and groping, then Stink tearing her Donna Karan blouse in two, and eventually stripping her naked. Their very first mix? Downward

50

doggie on her office floor. It was a Friday, just like today, that turned into endless fornication.

"Where'd you get those shoes?" Stink asked as soon as he'd ended his call. His eyes had been fixated on her since she exited the bathroom.

"Harvey Nichols in London. $500, why?" she replied while fastening the straps on her bedazzled Christian Louboutin pumps to her ankles, the fading sunlight creeping through the third floor window magnifying her pretty face and still bare chest.

When she looked up, Stink was taking his timepiece off, not even a foot from where she was standing. He said, "Looks like something my wife might like."

Shandy was about to put her mouth on his flaccid pipe, see if she could get it back up and kiss him all over, until she heard that. Instead, she slipped back into her bra, fastened the clasp at her cleavage. "Not sure they'd look as good on a size ten as they do on a size six."

"You are lucky you work for me, and I love the way your tight twat adjusts to my every thrust."

Shandy situated herself in her black pencil skirt, peach blouse and jacket, and said, "Was that a compliment or a contemplated threat?"

"Both," Stink bristled on his way to the bath area. "I'm more frightened than I am flattered!" she shouted thinking he was gonna shut the door behind him. But he didn't. He turned the shower on, stuck his head out the door and shouted back, "I don't believe you!"

Shandy gazed until she made eye contact with her forlorn lover before he could pull his head back into the bathroom. "You're right! I may've gone to school for journalism, and I might not be from Harlem, and I'm not your first choice -- but I can hold my own," she informed him, her face just inches from his now.

Stink watched as she spoke. As she fluttered her dark and thickened lashes she asked, "And what do you mean, sometimes a niggah be needing reassurance?"

Stink pulled his head back playing the roll of a shy kid, and that type of modesty just titillated Shandy. Stink had a resume that allowed him the authority to be cocky and arrogant, drunk with conceit and egotistical. Street cats and entertainers were nearly synonymous. They wanted to be each other. She loathed many of her clients with street ties, the wannabes. The ones who lacked the courage to be themselves. Not Stink though, Shandy mused, not my Stink.

"Sometimes I need to be reminded that I'm above average."

"You know what?" She came into the bathroom, rested her hip on the sink and watched as Stink showered. "You're the kind of guy who can smack a girl on her behind and when she turns around be left to wonder whether to curse your ass out or thank you for noticing her."

Stink smiled, almost caring and benevolent, her words of wisdom and feel of worldwise, finishing off what her sex hadn't. Shandy was a thrill to be around and to work with. Stink loved her scent, her style, her fearless aura, her sexuality, and most of all, the way she looked at him.

He dried himself off feeling complete, and trying to regain his composure. There was no way he was going to let her know the type of affect she had on him mentally and emotionally. Unfortunately for him, the mirth was still visible in the corners of his mouth as he tried to move pass Shandy. She eased over to his

52

vibrant smile, kissed him, then grabbed the rest of her things and headed for the door.

Ogling he well rounded derriere, Stink said, "Does your loving boyfriend know that you think monogamy is for birds?"

She wasn't completely committed to the theory, but she had to pretend to be to make her and Stink make sense. After all, Stink was married, and she was the side piece. "No," she answered in a hushed tone.

"Or that you get a thrill out of fucking a gangsta, then going home to cuddle and coddle with him?"

"So fucking arrogant," she said shaking her head.

"That wasn't the question, Miss Walton."

"Actually it's not you that keeps me coming back." She paused for effect. "It's the view of New York's cosmopolitan flare from this balcony. It's just so beautiful."

"And for the past two months I thought it was what I do to you on that balcony," he told her slipping back in to his clothes. "Guess I thought wrong."

As forthcoming as Shandy was, she couldn't muster the guts to verbalize her truest feelings, the fascination, the unbridled passion. Stink was a cure to her constant feel of disappointment and loneliness, a fixation that was taking residence in her soul. But in the rear of her subconscious she didn't see a future for them. At least one that surpassed secrecy. Outside in the corridor of the hotel, Shandy saw no one. "How much longer do you think we can do this?" she wondered out loud.

"I don't know," Stink replied watching her closely, the best fusion of class and sass he'd ever seen. "I can't call it, so I try not to think about it."

"Text me," she urged, backpedalling towards the elevator.

Stink nodded. And once again they left the suite and all its fabulous amenities behind minutes apart. In just a few strides they were in the thick of Times Square, which was no longer the Deuce, but a theme park. No hookers with track marks running up and down her arms. No whores with thongs and pimps way up their assess. No johns jonesing. No peep shows. MTV and Mickey Mouse were now the main attractions.

Shandy headed up to her 6th Avenue office, and Stink towards the Theater District where he'd parked up. Deep inside Shandy wished she and Stink were the blushing couple a few feet from her unable to keep their hands off each other. She wished they could practice public displays of affection. And before he knew it, Stink was drumming his fingertips on the steering wheel of his SUV, having just exited the underground garage and running right into a red light. In no rush, he took the long way back to New Jersey.

CHAPTER SIX

It was a little after midnight when Stink's headlights lit up the driveway of his home, the thought of his compulsive sexual behavior no longer the only thing on his mind. He would've been home sooner, but after leaving Muse Hotel he shot up to Harlem. The streets were overflowed with familiar faces, everybody trying to make something happen. And Stink was known for making things happen. If it wasn't getting you in the hottest cars in the 90s, it was getting you the best prices on coke.

These days it was other shit. Stink was the man. You wanna get in the rap game, holla at Stink. You got an idea for a movie, holla at Stink. You trying to shake your ass for money, holla at Stink. But what had fallen on his ears prior to parking at his Pallisades abode, he could've never expected.

He had his hands in his pockets, two of his trusted comrades close by, and an approachable smile on his face. A black on black BMW pulled up, and erased all that. It was some young cat he knew from the Polo Grounds, probably just pushing twenty, and his right hand occupying the 7-series. Not disrespectful, but definitely overly aggressive, the kid said, "Stink, we gotta rap, skrap."

"About what?" Stink quizzed, his head cocked to the side and his hands now at his side.

Those that knew they weren't suppose to be in the know, and knew it be best to mind their own business stepped off. When they did the kid said, "Where that nigga Zest at?"

"Why what's poppin?"

The kid touched the bridge of his nose, looked around like he was six-five when he was barely five-five. "More or less, that nigga ain't answering his phone."

Now Stink's shooters were getting pissed. Could see it all in their posture, and the way their breathing patterns suddenly changed. Stink said, "And you're telling me this why?"

"I'm saying, I know he ain't Homie. But ain't y'all partners."

"What's your name again?", Stink quizzed.

"Five!" the kid snapped nodding his head.

"Understand me and understand me clear Five, that's my man. Our business affairs, are not public information. Follow me?"

The kid nodded, his brows furrowed, shoulders hunched.

Guess that was to show that he was listening, but he wasn't done talking.

"And what is it that you want to tell him anyway?"

"That he better have my bricks, or bring my money back."

Before Stink could respond, the kid added, "He took a bunch of our money."

"When?!" asked Stink, eyeing both kids closely.

"Last week. I put that on my pops."

"How much money we talking about?" That was Stink.

"Two hundred of mine--

The second kid to dismount the 7-series said, "I met the nigga under the ridge on 155th last week to grab two of them things. Them shits was wrapped, Vaseline and ran, felt right and all that. But when I got to the spot, busted them open -- it was two erotic novels. Word up!" This kid was heavy set and had some height to him.

"First time y'all ever did business?"

"Nah, homie. That's why I'm bugging right now. What he think, niggas is pussy?" Five spat. "Over my dead pops body!" That saying had got the kid famous. "Over my dead pops body."

And Stink knew that. Overall it was an act of aggression. A sign of disrespect. The last five years of the 90s belonged to Stink and his crew. And Zest was part of that crew. Everybody knew it. He was the best man at Stink's wedding. And more than anything, Stink wanted to know where Zest was, and what was really good with him. "If I hear from him, I'll see what's poppin'."

That wasn't enough, and Stink knew it. $250k in the ghetto was considered wealth. And fooling with a nigga's paper was considered suicide. The driver of the BMW said, "Here's my number." He'd already had it written down, which made Stink ask, "How'd you know you were gonna see me?"

"I was at your press conference earlier, but it wasn't the time. And then my lil bitch told me you was out here on the Ave."

Stink left there as soon as they did. He was salty, lips curled up and mashing the gas. No one seemed to know where Zest was, and he wasn't answering his phone. Straight to voice mail. The last known address still belonged to him, but the door man said he hadn't seen Zest.

Rosa's car wasn't back yet, and that didn't seem to bother him. He sat his keys on the island separating the kitchen and living room, looked around. He saw hardwood floors, Italian leather, imported curtains, a gas fireplace, stainless steel appliances, a brick pizza oven, a dining table made to seat ten, and enough frozen memories to last a couple life times. There was a photo of he and Zest in tuxedos. Stink had made a lot of money with Zest.

This was a long ways from the Harlem flat he watched many Christmas's walk out of and get sold to the block boss. Look at him now. Stink had too much time to reflect.

Uncut was about to come on when Rosa strolled in to find Stink in bed, remote in hand. He said, "What poppin?"

And she replied, "It was real busy tonight."

Rosa peeped the disdain, but paid it no mind. Instead, she stripped, leaving her clothing in a pile on the carpet at the foot of the bed, sauntered off towards the shower holding her breath. By the time the water hit her flesh, Stink's favorite video was on. And then his phone chirped. Somebody had a number for Zest.

Within minutes Stink had Zest's attention.

"Yeah, it's true," Zest said.

"But why?"

"Lost the connect."

Stink sat up. "You don't owe them?"

"Nah, nah; They took a hit, and I couldn't get no consignment. I'm good though."

"Them niggas is tight."

"The little nigga talking about some over his dead pops."

"What up, you good right?"

"Yeah, yeah."

"Then fuck them."

The call ended shortly after, with Zest saying, "I'll be in town soon.   Real soon."

Rosa returned just as Stink sat his phone down. Five-nine, nearly-six feet on stilettos, 160 pounds of Latina lusciousness. About a foot of dark and curly hair that glistened whether wet or dry fell past her shoulders. And she had a set of lips that were made for kissing, and a face many would find something interesting about. But it was her neckline, collarbone and breasts she loved most about her physical features.

"How did the press conference go?"

"Rough. Some shit about some photos came up."

"What photos?"

"Me leaving a restaurant--"

"Overall though?"

"Good. What up, you all right?" asked Stink. Of course she was!

Once upon a time Rosa believed in the fantasy fairy tale romance. Believed she would enjoy a lasting love like the kind her parents shared. But that all changed a couple of years ago when reality struck.

Rosa was just beginning her third summer fling in two years, a lusty tryst no one could've predicted. With time shares in the Poconos, Puerto Rico, and South Beach, and a husband she could barely talk to, it seemed ideal to be drinking and boning and living in the lap of lust with a part-time lover. The idea had come from the seductive block buster Unfaithful. And those temporary and pleasurable arrangements were actually what helped her keep her cool, her sanity, from dying from a broken heart.

She laughed inside thinking of how bold and brazen it was of her to bare all in front of her husband knowing that had he been looking to pop her, she couldn't deny him, and he would've not only found her vagina moist, but also a little loose. No adulteress in the history of infidelity would've been so daring. For her, it was a suspicion killer. If he ever got suspicious, there would be a killing.

She slipped into a silk teddy Stink had bought her when times were better, and slipped into bed. There they lay, only a few inches separating them, both worlds apart though. Proof that money wasn't everything. Rosa peeked over and said, "I love you."

"Love you," Stink replied, his eyes nowhere in particular

CHAPTER SEVEN

Zest was blessed. Unlike his cousin Capri, he'd managed to ward off the evils of law enforcement. A traffic stop here, a minor arrest there, but the Major Crimes Unit of Manhattan knew very little, if anything, about the equally as evil Hayward. Short and stout with a neatly shaven baldy, and a goatee, he had a lot more to be thankful for than his good looks and good fortune.

There was a blackness to his soul, demons he fought more than he'd like to. Witnessing his first love, Princess Q's life get cut short and not be able to do a damn thing about it, had its effects. But more than anything -- the many murders he participated in or committed singlehandedly. The unruly biker, the two court officers, Destro, the lady who reminded him of his own mother, Sonny... Those were the ones that stuck out, they would never leave his conscience. And then all the homeboys lost in their battle for supremacy. Nickels, Bones, Lux, 730, BB... Almost a decade had passed, but that feeling wouldn't fade. He was surrounded by death.

Every once in a while Action would even come to mind. The battle for supremacy. He had it all. Privilege and power, for a long time. And then, it was over.

Zest was at the Phipps Plaza, located in the Buckhead section of Atlanta, GA when his phone chirped, and it was made clear that Stink was checking for him. As he had exited the mall's underground parking lot in a Saab station wagon right off Peachtree, he had requested Stink's new number and promised he'd get with him soon as possible.

He was tired of taking risk, and just a week ago he thought he was taking his last. It had been a rough week, leading up to his departure. Robbery after robbery, larceny and then some. He had started with some kid named Mouse.

When he had kicked the door in; Mouse, a Yonkers resident with a mean heroin flow, was in bed with his latest piece of skin, a sexy little snow bunny from Westchester, NY. That was the new phenom, white girls. Niggahs were sleeping with them, putting babies in them, and all that. This one had lustrous blond hair, a tight body, sleep -- in the nude. Mouse had the look of the lost and found in his eyes when he noticed Zest reaching for his neck. "I just want what's available, you can keep the rest."

He skated out of there with almost thirty in cash, and was on to the next.

In the nearby borough of the Bronx, not far from where he'd been paying rent these days. Dust was popping again, and it wasn't like crack where everybody had it. Jet fuel was hard to come by, and if you did get it, you still needed to know what you were doing. Two liters were going for almost two grand. And this, used-to be pimp was a wholesaler. Zest had got word that police were squeezing him and immediately thought he could use the money more.

Zest had let himself in to the small window leading out to the fire escape while they sat high off their very own supply.

Dust wasn't for everyone, but especially potential robbery victims. When he saw them in a daze watching Monster's Ball, he knew this would be a piece of pie. Within minutes of his entry and the sight of his big gun they offered up   the product. But Zest didn't want that, he was out the game officially. He wanted cash.

"Ain't no cash here man!" the slender pimp fellow pled.

"I'm ask one more time--" Zest snapped from behind his mask.

The man again insisted there was no money on hand. So Zest pulled a clear plastic bag from his waistline which was folded up very neatly, and yanked it down over the guy's girlfriend's head. She was a looker too, even spaced out of her mind. The sexy little chocolate cupcake of a chick struggled as best she could, but he so easily wrapped a shoestring around her sleek neck completely packing her head in the bag. The guy watched in disbelief as her facial expression quickly changed. She was past the verge of fear. And so was her pimp. If never before, the pimp felt a connection to the young runaway. Not love or affection, but regret for not giving her her true worth.

"The sink, it lifts up!" he screamed.

Zest relinquished her, then tied them both up. When he dismantled the sink, his phone continuously buzzed. The young niggas about them bricks. The mind frame he was in was the wrong time for anybody to be mentioning money to him. When he finally did remove the stash from the sink deposit, it was nowhere near where he thought it would be. Nice, but the money those young cats were trying to flip was ten times as nice. So he decided to link up with them before he headed south.

63

In the process of pulling that lick off, he didn't know that someone had heard all the commotion and called the police. And when the address came over the dispatch, the cops that were extorting him decided to swing by. Either he had been just unbelievably careful or extremely lucky.

It was the former!

Zest had figured out escape routes, and backup plans, ins and outs of every hood he entered. One of the escape routes involved jumping roofs, taking him from one strip to the next. Which is what he had to do to escape this one.

As he walked to his rent al that night, he thought of his fall. With the exception of bad spending habits and a gambling addiction that had him partying in Vegas every other weekend, it was to no fault of his own. It was like the great depression when Wall Street crashed. His connect had lost their leader back in Mexico, and everyone close to him. They were left in America unemployed, and Zest with a loath for the game. He was getting 100 bricks at a time, paying them when he was finished, and subconsciously believed that would last forever. That's when he started planning for his new future.

Today his interests, personally and concerning capital ventures were different. He had invested in an adult film company with a pornographic magazine entitled the same name. Ass Appointments. He was tapping into a new kind of power, the kind that got him friendly with pro football players, music producers, NBA champs, and some of the finest ass in the world.

He didn't care about settling scores anymore, or what the fuck was going on in New York. Until he heard Stink was checking for him, and what it was about.

CHAPTER EIGHT

"Mom, please hurry up!" Little Olivia bellowed looking up at her mother. She had some impatience in her voice and urgency in her eyes, Christine noticed.

She saw so much of herself in the seven-year-old.

Well, she didn't grow up with diamonds on her neck and in her ears, or the best kid clothes money could buy, but she too was very antsy and energetic and inquisitive just like her daughter. "Why? You gotta use the bathroom again?"

"No!"

"Then, what is it?"

It was almost a whisper. "My friend's gonna be mad if I'm late mom."

Christine went from zero to sixty in three seconds -- "What fucking friend???" She thought her daughter was getting a little loonie on her. "Child please, your father is gonna spaz if I don't get this stuff mailed out today. They were five 35 pound packages she had to have shipped containing mix-tapes, toiletries, Timbs, and nonperishable foods. One was for Capri, the other four were for his comrades. Two she knew of, met on family visits, and the other two she knew nothing about. What

said, his eyes taking in all the beauty.

"Hi, Stink," the chorus replied, their goods jiggling and wiggling a little.

His watch read 8:20. "Everyone pay their twenty-five dollar deductible up front?"

All except one had. Every once in a while she'd do that. Stink nodded to her response, said, "My office."

The Ruby Red office was nothing like the one over at the Auto Sound. But is was fit for business. This kind of business. With the exception of video surveillance, no records were kept. Two leather love seats sat on either side, then there was a desk where 10 inch monitors gave clear footage of the place. With both his hands painted on the desktop, Stink was now looking at all the card dealers, the bartender, the house men shaking the dice, the back exit, the front door, and finally the VIP section which resembled department store dressing rooms.

As he sat in one of the swivel chairs, spun around, 360, he heard knuckles rapping on the office door. "Come in!" said Stink planting his feet firmly. It was the shorty. She peeked behind her, then stepped in and shut the door. Stink was a great lover, he could maintain an erection longer than any cat she had ever encountered, and she relished every opportunity she got with him. "Azure, right?" Stink said. He knew her name, it was just a little game the two played.

"Yes," she gushed, playing the bashful role. Only problem with that – she was now topless, just a sliver of thong covering her genitalia, and sin was written all in her swag. Stink was rock-hard and ready to pop something. She wasn't just extremely arousing and gravity to the eyes, but she was smart, and had

70

provided Stink with some of his deepest conversations. She was the woman from Megu.

He was about to reach out and touch her when over the intercom came: "Boss, Soup wanna know if its enough people for a good poker game tonight?"

"We ain't even open yet!"

"Soup's on the phone!"

Stink thought of everyone who would be there, the competition, the amount to buy in. Texas, Omaha, Pineapple, Five Card Stud, Straight Seven... "Yeah!"

"Copy, copy!" the employee replied.

"Now back to you," Stink snickered rubbing his hands together.

Azure's breasts weren't too big or too small. Her waist was tapered and her hips and thighs benefited perfectly. She had long thick hair, which was a natural sandy color. She was tall and fit, plump in the butt, not a stretch mark in sight. Her face formed into pretty smiles at will, and made the best sexual expressions he'd ever seen. But what Stink liked most about her figure was her washboard stomach. Every bitch he was popping could hold their own, but the stomach took sexiness to another level.

She said, "I've been dying to see you since the other day!"

"How's school?" Stink asked while pulling her to him.

"Maintaining my 4.0," she told him as she sat in his lap.

"You already know." Stink genuinely cared about her. Azure was special to him in her own way. She had never interacted sexually with a man on the premises other than Stink. And it was their little secret. Stink had planned to set her out with some loot to finish up at NYU. That's how deep her story was, and how much he wanted to see her succeed. But Azure refused, figuring

71

she could pay and pave her own way off what little fantasies she did fulfill at the club. It wasn't ideal, or the grandest of ambitions, but she saw the Ruby Red as she and Stink's getaway. That's it. There, she was the only woman who mattered to him.

Her arms were draped around Stink's neck, her hands caressing the back of his head as she said, "I've admired you since I was in the ninth grade. Whenever I heard you horn on your convertible red Lex coupe, I'd run to my living room window, the only one with a view to 115th Street, just to get a glimpse of you. You probably didn't even know I existed back then..."

Stink said, "I didn't." He was holding onto her backside like it would fall off the face of the earth if he had let it go. Her gray eyes caught his and held, and she told him, "I loved the way you walked and talked, the authority you had. And I love the way you hold me."

"I love the way you talk that legal shit," Stink replied caressing the soft skin on her behind. "You're gonna be a great lawyer one day."

There was no music on, but they didn't need it. They had their own mood and melody going. "I always knew you'd go on to do great things," she told him in a whispered falsetto.

His voice now a staccato cadence, he said, "I appreciate that, babygirl."

A marriage counselor would render Stink a sex addict. And a life coach would, outside of her being a student at a prestigious university, consider Azure a bad decision maker. But they didn't come from the land of counselors and life coaches, they were from the ghetto where fantasies were acted upon.

Azure kissed Stink, nicely. Her full lips loving his. He was about to run his mouth all over her bare breasts. But two things happened.

The door was open for business!

And Stink noticed Iris on one of the monitors, mingling and kissing the cheeks of the girls she knew. Stink kissed both nipples, told her, "See you later. Me and you, right here."

Azure left and Iris arrived two minutes later. She stuck her hand out and Stink kissed it. "And to what do I owe this pleasure?" he asked.

"First, you look good. Haven't seen you in a minute," she responded. "Now, I went to see Capri, and he said them kids is part of the new wave, and that as far as he's concerned they can bite a power line."

"The Five cat?"

Iris nodded. "Next, I got dude right where we want him."

"We want him alive."

"He will be," Iris said grinning. "This nigga had the nerve to take me to your wife's spot. Real elegant. You should be proud of her."

"When y'all 'pose to like up again?"

"This weekend. He think I'ma give him some pussy, let him fuck me in my ass and all that."

"I've been waiting on this revenge for a long time. We -- I should say."

Their eyes met. "Yes, we. Us!"

Iris was wearing a sexy cat suit, panther black, with some peep-toe pumps the same color. If Capri wasn't so fucked up about Iris, Stink would've tested the waters, swam all up in her. As he was having that secret moment, Iris said, "I'm thinking about getting away from here once Capri gets out. I hear

"Why? Thought the rules were, bring a friend--"

Stink's lips curled up into his mouth, then he said, "He is not welcomed here."

"Why?" Lansky said, in no mood to be treated like some little twirp. This wasn't the 90s and his name did sound like something now too. But he didn't want Stink's wrath, still people were watching even if they couldn't hear what he was saying.

"He and Zest got something going on," Stink shot in Lansky's ear. "What he didn't tell you? No because he used you to see where I stood in the whole fucking thing."

"Nah, he didn't say--"

"Of course he didn't." Stink paused, because had he not, he would have slapped Lansky to the ground. "He's playing you. Listen ... more is suppose to change your conditions, not the way you fucking move. Don't forget where you come from."

Lansky was stuck. And he really liked Five. "Stink," he said, "that's my bad, Blood."

Five stood to the side taking it all in. He knew who Stink was, followed his story through the 90s, through the 2000s. Knew he was very tight with Capri. Part of the first wave of the revolutionary reflection that changed the culture here in New York City. So he wasn't tripping. Not yet. There was no doubt in his mind that he would get back what Zest had taken. He had what is called chutzpa! His father had left him with it. And over his father's dead body would anybody take it from him.

Stink saw Five alone and rather mellow, so he toned it down on Lansky, but not off. As he was giving Lansky the low down, something Lansky couldn't even believe, having worked with Zest for several years in the past, Five had disappeared from his periphery. Then Rita J. pulled up on them, said, "Stink this is from Five."

"Tell him I don't want it." I don't want him here, is what Stink really wanted to say. But since it would be Five's last time in there ever, he kept it to himself. But he wasn't excepting the bottle. This wasn't Carlita's Way, and he wasn't Benny Blanco from the Bronx.

"Okay," she said with a smile then about-faced.

Five thought he could dig it, Stink had chosen a side. He got two g lasses from the barmaid, and found him a honey to mack with. Either he was already drunk, or he couldn't see the revulsion on her face. The lighting was perfect, bright red, so he saw her face. But is was the red heart shaped pasties hiding her nipples1 and the heart shaped ass that had him. She didn't have on any makeup, and she didn't need it. She was the best thing smoking in the club, and the only one he hadn't seen putting herself out there, though all the girls had some class about them. I wanna bust her ass, Five thought feverishly. He envisioned his throbbing penis gliding over her breasts, neckline and chin, slowly passing over her eyes, nose and lips, before being rammed in her mouth.

Five beckoned for the girl, and she got to him in no hurry. She gave him a dance, no contact, which he couldn't understand.

But her body was so crazy and her eyes so sexy that he still blessed her. As she was strutting off in her red platforms, Five said, "Fuck you, bitch! Don't let me catch you--"

"Or what?" Stink wanted to know. Before Five could recover, explain, Stink said, "He gotta go. Now!"

The bouncers always felt like they were in a foreign land, M-16s in their clutches. That military experience. And it showed when they gripped Five's little as up. He was quick though, spinning out of their grasps. "Fuck I do?" he asked Stink.

The head bouncer reached for his stun gun. He wanted to hit Five, let that thing crackle with jolts. He could already smell the ozone!

"Aiight, I'm out. But I put that on my dead pops. Ya man better have my shit!"

"Yeah, whatever. I know, you gotta put it on ya dead pops to hype ya little ass up!"

He couldn't hear Stink, the music was too loud now. Still, he said, on his way out, "On my dead pops!"

$ $ $

Five swung his boyish frame from his BMW, which he had parked discreetly on Sedgwick Avenue in the western section of the Bronx. He was still having problems digesting the way he had been treated at the Ruby Red, by someone he once idolized, and in some ways still looked up to. He'd been tossed out of better places for less, but never was he consumed with this type of hatred. There was only one way to relieve himself.

As he locked up he thought about the reason for the dislike, something, anything that made the least bit of sense.

He hadn't taken Zest's money, Zest had taken his, right? Had it been anyone else, there would've been no talking. Anyone else. Anyone-fucking-else! Bang! Bang!! Straight like that!

He needed some release, something to take his mind off Stink's arrogant ass. He needed someone else to exert his will on. That's what he did, it was his secret. Standing on the shiny-wet asphalt, evidence of an earlier downpour, he looked around. This was the homeland of a chick he'd been tracking for a while, spying whenever he had some free time. A sassy one with a lot going for herself. Long hair, bright eyes, and a bright future. She didn't know much about him though, if anything. There she was, slender and sleek with a black umbrella in her right hand. She was smiling about something, and Five found that to be intriguing. A smile was like a form of charity, until someone took it away.

There were towering buildings throughout the neighborhood, security in the lobbies, but she lived in a five story tenement with rusty hinges on the front gate. The first time he'd noticed her was at a fashion show at the Apollo where she modeled for a budding designer, and then a party at a Harlem bowling alley that she hosted. She had some sexy ass legs and dreamy eyes, to say the least. Seemed average, approachable, but she shut him down. He was used to being the chosen one, only he failed to realize those young dames who were choosing him really didn't have a clue of what they wanted. And most of the time it wasn't him anyway, it was what he had. He didn't take rejection lightly, it brought the worse out of him. People knew it, especially in his neighborhood, so he got his way a lot. But no one had him under this act.

As the young female got closer, he became more aroused, and what he'd been willing to pay Stink's sexy law student for, he was about to take for nothing. The click-clack of her shoes got closer and closer, until she strutted right past him. He expected it. She smells delicious, he thought, even better than that bitch at the Ruby Red! She turned into the building, and just as the front door was shutting, Five stepped in. Initially, he planned to follow Azure home, ruin her ass, but the club had closed and she never emerged. Neither did Stink. Thought maybe they'd exited through the back. That's when he started cruising.

Five headed for the stairs, bypassing Sexy Legs. She was still

smiling, obviously happy about something. Hardly noticed when
Five turned back, until she was being forced into the open
elevator. Instinct said scream, but Five said, "I just want the
bush." In a real hush, hush tone. "Now what floor are we going
to? Don't say it, just hit it. I can't stand the sound of your voice."

She wondered where she knew him from and why he doing
this to her, while tapping the button with the number 4 on it. The
elevator ascended and so did Five's free hand -- right up her skirt.
She wished she hadn't been beefing with her boyfriend, that she
didn't live alone, that the nicotine on Five's breath wasn't so close
to her nostrils. She could feel his fingertips invading her, and
winced with the touch. Fear filled her once fearless eyes. Five
grinned putting the suckle from her vagina to his nostrils.
"Sweet," he said, his eyes half mast and his identity still a
mystery. She could feel cold steel in her lower back, his gun, and
warmth on her inner thigh, his erection. The elevator door flew
open and the floor she resided on stared back at her. She yelped
when she saw the shadow of someone sitting on the stairs. Her
eyes welled up thinking there might be two of them. Two against
one. Un-consensual sex with two unwanted predators.

Five was just a little taller than her 5'3" stature, his arm
wrapped around her throat. "Our stop," he chuckled, wanting
badly to tell her why he had chosen her. But then he'd have to kill
her. "Slow. There's no rush, we have all night," he told her while
allowing her sensual scent to tickle his beak. And he did have a
beak, with his hawk-like features. What luck to have. She
couldn't believe her eyes. The shadow belonged to her boyfriend.
He'd come unexpectedly. And he had no sense at times.

"Lava, he has a gun," she whimpered as he rose from his
crouching position, shock in his eyes. But there was nothing he

could do. He didn't stand a chance. The shots were loud, and
direct hits. Two to the chest. For the girl this was far more
horrific than force entry. Her lover was gasping as blood rushed
from his wounds and his mouth, grasping his chest as death's
angels swooped in. Five could still hear the girl's cries as he sped
away. He knew this feeling already, and very well, yet he
couldn't believe the chain of events. A night of fun had turned
deadly!

CHAPTER TEN

The next morning Stink's face was on New York 1 News.
Not the face from the Ruby Red, his other face. Not the shooting
death on. Sedgwick Avenue, or the attempted rape victim telling
her story. Not coverage of the NBA finals. Not the economy.
Stink's black ass! Correspondents from several media outlets,
along with veteran activists, were on to critique and assess the
press conference concerning Stink's nonprofit organization and
its focus.

"I mean, even if that's the case, everyone has some good in
them. Hey, the Kennedys weren't always pillars of our society,"
said one activist known for her human rights work.

"The Clinton Chronicles depict someone other than the
governor we elected to Office," another brown skinned activist
offered in turn. "Every sinner has a past and every saint has a
future I guess is what we're here saying today, and that is the
general feeling of everyone on this panel."

Now they comparing this nigga to presidents!, Five snapped,
pitching his remote control at the big wide screen. He'd been
drinking all night. No sleep. Pacing the confines of his mama's
efficiency, thinking about his money and his next move. Yeah,
Five was one of them fast life cats holding residence at his
mama's crib. Scared to leave the nest. Infuriated, he walked over
to the window and glared out, took on the sun until his young

84

eyes could take no more. With a bottle of Vodka in tow, he spun around right into the bosom of his mama.

"Boy, what the fuck is wrong with you? Only time you home this time of day is when your ass is hiding out! Now what you done did, negro? And who you did it to?" she jabbed looking him up and down. "Gimme some money," she quickly followed up with.

His mother, Maliah Anthony, was one of those moms who made kids wonder was she to blame for what they'd become. She'd never really been there for him, only a kid herself at the time of his birth. She was hardly ever around, and embraced the fact that he addressed her as Maliah instead of mommy. Fashion statements was her focus, and worrying about what people thought about her. At age 36 today, she was the exact same way, and showed no signs of change. He had never even seen her with his father, but every time he turned around she had a new nigga in the crib. One thing for sure, she was fly, and pretty. As he flared at this ghetto fab lady, his stomach weakened. He thought of the rumors that were swirling when he was in the eleventh grade; his mama fucking some nigga just a couple years older than him. She was 31, and the kid was 19. Her justification was, "He's getting' it!" Referring to money.

Five realized the only person to ever give a fuck about him was his pop. He never met his maternal or paternal grandparents, and was oblivious to his ancestry. Just a child of the ghetto, only direction, the street corner or the park bench. He threw the wad in his pocket at his mama, shouting profanities, then spent the rest of that afternoon at his father's gravesite.

About two days later the strangest thing happened. Five was hold up in a project apartment with his cronies playing some video game that had their undivided attention. There was four in total, boots off, and a stripper Five had brought home the night before. She reminded him of the lead in Nelly's controversial music video, Tip Drill. When it first aired he never missed an episode of BET's late night show. She danced, adding a feminine feel to the testosterone-filled cubby hole, while they passed the time gambling on NBA Live.

Five wanted to win one more game then retreat to the back of the room and exploit his dancing acquaintance's greed. He palmed her soft ass, kissed her hip, then grinned. As he went for a feel of her C-cup, his phone chirped. It was a local fool. And it went something like this: "Yo, baby boy! Somebody was just fucking with that mean whip of yours. The alarm went off, then it went off."

No one knew about the events from the day before, how he'd been thrown out the Red Ruby, or what happened after that. He rose to his feet wondering could there be a connection. He said, "What you mean?"

"The shit was making noise, then it stopped."

"Is anything broke? Windows, headlights?"

This ain't the work of a woman," the caller said, his voice flooded with signs of wisdom and knowledge. "Somebody's in the front seat."

"WHO?"

"I don't know. I was in the store--"

"And somebody's in the front seat right now?" Five bristled.

"Yeah -- man! Behind the muthafuckin wheel."

Five hung up on the caller and thought for a brief moment. All eyes were on him as he palmed his heat. The guy reporting to him was a trusted smoker, one of his very first licks, a fiend instrumental in his climb from the bottom. This fiend had secrets, things he shouldn't know. The type of shit prosecutors pay handsomely for. He'd seen Five rape a girl, and kill a man. Two isolated incidents, but equally treacherous. The girl had been playing on his emotions, taking his money with no true intentions of ever putting out. So one night Five waited in her building and took her down at gun point in a back stairwell. Took his time too, real sinister like. A year later, just a towering building away, a rival was shot in the back fleeing a rapid fire. Five, the son of a hard headed nigga, learned of the watchful eyes the way no one wishes to. The fiend had told Five's father days before his father got his chest sent through his back, and the bottom half of his jaw tagged to a wall. And then, there was only two people who knew. And time, as always, was the supreme test. Five's father was buried three years ago. He could trust that the fool was being truthful, right? And not trying to set him up, right? After all, his secrets were safe.

He cocked his hammer anyway!

"Somebody's in my fucking car!" he informed his boys. "Do not shoot the muthafucker in my car," he ordered and then they descended to the streets.

$ $ $

Zest was in town. In all black fatigues, chukka boots and a dark brim. Taking money, of course. He   had   two   country bammers with him who were just as thankful to Stink as Zest was for representing the truest code of loyalty. They were under the 155th Street Bridge in a dark sedan leaned back and unnoticeable. Zest's blood was boiling. He hadn't been in this mode in quite some time. But he was a goon for real. Through

87

and through. And when he popped off, he didn't miss. Had niggas forgotten? Or was the new jacks just disregarding history? The clock on the dash read 11:15 p.m. So far everything was going accordingly.

"You cats were dead serious when y'all said y'all didn't mind getting y'all hands dirty, huh?"

They were feeling Zest, both Atlanta natives, for different reasons. The one in the passenger seat said, "We got a lot more than our hands dirty."

"Ain't that right?" the one in the back seat added, and they all busted out laughing.

Just before they'd boarded the flight to Kennedy, they were partying in a sprawling mansion where they were to finish off the photo shoot for the first issue of Ass Appointments the next week. They recalled sitting back watching Zest as he mingled effortlessly with the street cats, the tax payers and one of the baddest women in Georgia.

Zest recalled watching from a distance as her luscious lips moved, pondering the softness of them touching his flesh. She had a reputation for dating heavy hitters and trouble makers, so Zest fit the mode. A beautiful set of blue icy eyes that seemed intelligent peered from her face, scanning the room. There was a little puffiness to them, and they were slightly baggy, but still a sight to see. Eventually Zest had approached her, and he didn't have to boast, she knew it, that he was a gangsta. Arguably one of the reigning gangstas.

The party got louder, more crowded, vulgar and... still Zest felt like he couldn't take his eyes away from her. The longer he gazed, the more he came to the realization that this woman was stunning in the way those 20 million a movie actresses were.

Finally a chick who can replace Princess, he thought.

He tried not to be rude in a stylish two piece suit, but the truth of the matter was he was rude. "When I get back from New York, I'm taking you away," he had said.

"What's in New York?" she asked, this sexy undertone caressing his ear.

Just as he thought of the lie he'd made up, the guy sitting next to him said, "What made you think of some wild shit like that, Zee?"

Zest was going by Zee in the Dirty South. He said, "Some fly shit he said to my man."

$ $ $

One by one, Five and his boys filed out of the building. There wasn't much going on. It was almost 11:30, and the night was jet black. The Beemer was about 100 feet away, one of the few cars parked on the side of the street they were on. The streetlamp just a few yards from the car provided just enough light for Five to see whoever was in his car. He could've sworn he'd seen the violator touching his things, moving around, looking for something to steal. Their steps became stomps as they neared one of their luxuries, a car that wasn't fully paid for. Five thought about what he was gonna do to the crook.

In a hasten move, Five stuck his arm out and said, "Wait! Lets wait for his ass to get out."

They backed up against the silver security gates of a storefront, posted up. Five minutes turned to 10. 10 to 20 minutes. Even the nigga who put Five on point was growing impatient from his watching position. He wanted his reward -- a few grams. He wasn't a crackhead, he did have standards.

Who would be so stupid?, everyone in the know wanted to know.

And without a word, Five backed his firepower out and converged on the car. His lips were pursed, his eyes slits, and there was malice in his every move. He considered the body in the building the other night a thing of luck, but this here would be a stroke of genius. This could be the momentum he needed. This could be his shining moment. The one murder he could talk about, and be praised for. Maybe then Stink would drink with him, make arrangements to have his money returned. Boy was he thinking big. And boy was he stuck on Stink. That's what envy does. It makes you hate the same things you love.

When he got to the driver's side door, he hit the alarm gaining access. Ready to put fire to that ass, right there on the pavement, shoot him until his clothes caug ht ablaze, Five snatched the car door open. He couldn't believe his eyes. His heart beat like a bass drum and his eyes nearly popped out his head. It was like a bad dream that he'd had before. More like a nightmare on a Harlem street. His gun slipped from his grasp as he noticed the ring, the watch. On a skeletal hand. There was a skeleton, long dead, in a snazzy suit, behind the wheel of his car. It was his father.   Five got dizzy, nearly lost his footing just as the sedan Zest was driving cruised pass. A goon's goon!

"Now!" Zest demanded, and just like that there was an explosion. It was loud, there was a forceful impact, and immediately red and blue flames engulfed the vehicle as smoke plumed from the inferno.

Even Zest couldn't believe what he was witnessing. Or, that he could be so vicious. A goon's goon! Maybe now he could get back behind his Atlanta desk.

CHAPTER ELEVEN

"There's explosives in Harlem now," Robert Moore, a detective with Harlem's major Crimes Unit, voiced as he dismounted his unmarked car.

A crime-lab van with dark windows was on the scene. A fire truck was pulling away. And then he noticed an EMS, Mortuary clearly visible on the back of the ambulance. And then a medical examiner in a plastic suit conferring with the crime-lab boys.

Detective Moore's brown eyes caught the medical examiner's and held on. They knew each other fairly well, worked together on several cases, and worked out together several times a week.

"You don't seem to be in any rush, Bob Moore!" the medical examiner chided.

"Hey, he's already dead right? He can't speak, and no one who can talk around here speaks, Ashford Banks," Detective Moore replied.

The medical examiner rose to a full stance, said, "You're not gonna believe this but the one behind the wheel – been dead."

Detective Moore's sidekick intervened -- "What do you mean been dead?"

"He's been dead for years."

Not one guy on the scene, on the right side of the law, had ever witnessed this kind of criminology. And quite frankly, not one of them wanted this case.

"Besides someone removing a corpse from its burial grounds and then abusing it, what else can you tell us about this...case?"

The smolder, the soot, the smoke -- nowhere near that magnitude -- but it made the officers on the scene remember 9/11. They were all part of that mayhem.

The med examiner said, "The had-been behind the wheel of the German machine isn't the owner of this melted flesh."

Bob Moore leaned into the toasted car without touching anything. He glanced over the skeletal remains, and went to the VIN number, the one thing he was sure would survive flames. He wanted to know who the car belonged to. He wanted to know whether that person was here. And whether that person was dead or somewhere dying. Judging by the conditions of the car, that person's condition couldn't be good. And then he wanted to know who'd done this, who was responsible, so he could put that ass away! Without surmising.

Bob Moore said, "There's a cemetery somewhere with a missing resident. Find out where!" A subordinate who was amongst the congregation trekked off to fill that order. And Bob Moore went on to say, "You've done this hundreds of times at least, Ashford -- anything crazier than this?"

"Ever hear of Anwar Action Outen?"

Bob Moore nodded.

"The bus terminal. Father and daughter gunned down. Fed shot dead. In the fed's vehicle -- a potential witness with multiple bones broken, snatched from her hospital bed, shot in her face. As the investigation ensues, two more found dead at the Outen

Compound out in Astoria, Queens. Six murdered same night, all connected somehow."

"Case still cold," Bob Moore said, his tone parallel with the rest of the somber feel of things.

"Actually, it just heated back up. This one made it all the way down to Quantico."

"The director of the FBI? No shit!"

"He definitely has office space there, not sure if he's involved though. I've always had a theory," Ashford Banks answered.

"I'd like to hear this being as though you've never mentioned it before," Bob Moore insisted. At the time of the Harlem power shift, he was part of a TNT team in the Bronx borough, just three years on the force. TNT was a task force that worked directly with the DA's office and reigned terror on the corner boys, their lookouts and lieutenants. He'd been part of a lot of busts and convictions, and had also seen the ugly side, drugs being planted, young kids jumping off bridges to escape, goons licking shots off roofs administering their brand of justice. He'd been pinned in a building once, nearly shoved over a rooftop before, a passenger in a car that flipped over in a high speed chase, but that was nothing compared to the madness in Harlem that boosted the crime rate that year. Being the history, buff that he was, he was eager for more.

"Here's my theory… something really bad happened…

"No shit!" Bob Moore snickered, his sarcasm not missed by anyone. At 200 pounds, five percent body fat, six foot, it would be hard to miss.

Equally as massive, Ashford Banks said, "The killings were vengeful. Revenge. The Action guy, he was pretty well off, parlayed illegitimate dealings into a pretty lucrative slab of real estate that included a lounge, furniture stores, car dealerships, among other things. The house out in Astoria, two mill easy. A car collection worth half a mill. He was on the FBI files for extortion, murder, tax evasion. The investigation stalled. His daughter was accepted to Syracuse, full scholarship. Both viciously shot dead in Harlem just a few feet from the lead agent in the investigation. Ballistics prove that Action fired the fatal shots of Trent Mccants, and then the lead goes cold, as far as forensics go. Now, his daughter, Patience Mccants, shot too, she's the only survivor..."

"I read that she was the sole survivor, in the New York Daily News, claims she didn't remember anything. Keep going, man!"

"The girl found dead in Mccants' vehicle, she was prepared to tell all. At nineteen, she knew enough to put everyone away. Snatched from a bed in the serious-condition ward alive, unauthorized ... found dead in the back seat of Mccants' car."

"The broken limbs, how --?"

"She was hit by a speeding car just a block from Saks Fifth, where her lover, a mid-level player in the west Bronx, was practically gutted like a pig."

"The Outen Compound?"

Ashford Banks said, "Action's underboss was found there shot to death with a gangbanger about half his age."

"The rest of his family?"

"Wife and kid son, vanished."

"The dead agent's daughter?" Bob Moore questioned.

"Left the country about a week after talking to the FBI."

"With a boyfriend?"

"No, her mom, a homicide cop with the Yonkers Police. But she did have a boyfriend. A boyfriend who lost both his parents to violence when he was just a kid."

"And where is he now?"

"Hey! Hey! Is anybody fucking working around here?!" That was the head of Major Crimes, a cat in his forties who could be cool when he wanted to be, and crass when necessary. Badges close to him called him X because he resembled the rapper DMX. He always dressed down, and in the latest. "Bombings in residential areas is a major crime!" And just as quick as he'd arrived, he had disappeared.

"The answer to your last question..." last I heard, he was state property."

Before Bob Moore could counter he was being told where the skeleton in the car had been stolen from. Upon digesting that info, he said, "Find out who this car is registered to."

Ashford Banks waited for the subordinate to vamoose, then said, "There's more." His eyes darted a bit. "He's supposed to be responsible for approximately thirty murders. The girl found in the agent's car, her sister was murder with an acquaintance outside the Bronx County Supreme court. This guy's cousin's girlfriend was found dead in her Central Park West apartment. Guess how?"

"After hearing what I've heard, I can't imagine."

"Explosives. Her face was blown up."

This was major. A break already. But it still felt like a surmise. Flimsy evidence that even J. Edgar Hoover's progeny could do nothing with.

Within the hour, Bob Moore had an owner to the car and the identity of the skeleton.

It was dark out, not even a sliver of the moon was visible, but Moore was on the move. The info led him to a tenement without an elevator, an old Harlem edifice, one of the first anchors erected here. He and his partner took the steps. Because there was no one dead on the scene, he rolled without reinforcement. The loud rapping of his knuckles on the apartment door brought forth the soft vocals of a woman. "Police. Open up. Just a few questions, please."

"I'm not dressed," the woman shouted back.

"Just a few questions," Bob Moore repeated.

The door creaked open, revealing 60 watts of light, and there stood a stunningly attractive woman in fire red panties and a pushup bra made of that pretty silk that Moore could see through easily. Five-foot-six, golden complexion, dark nipples, clean shaven. Moore couldn't help notice.

"And how can I help you fellas?"

"Are you Maliah?"

She said, "I am. What's up?"

"You live here?"

"I do."

"A lone?"

"With a friend."

"And you drive a BMW?"

"I'm   sorry, I don't drive. I'm a train kinda girl. Choo Choo."

Bob Moore cleared his throat. "Then who drives it?"

"My girlfriend Scarlet."

"Is she home?"

"No, I'm alone."

"I'm just a co-signer."

"Do you know where she can be found? She   might   be   in danger."

"She dances at a club in the Bronx. Can I ask what's goin on, sir?"

"Her car was found torched. Do you know if it was reported stolen or if anyone else drives it?"

"You mean, set on fire???"

Bob Moore could tell she didn't know what was going on.

"Actually, someone taped some explosives under the driver's seat, and tried to blow it off the earth," he told her.

"Was anyone hurt?"

"That's what we're trying to find out."

"Well, I'm fine. I was just relaxing," she said, more of a concerned look on her face and less wanton in her attitude.

"Do you know a man by the name of Danny Ray?"

"Yes," she pushed out.

"That's my son's father. He's dead, died right before the terrorist attack in Harlem."

"Ahhh, what club did you say she danced at?"

"I never said what club."

Bob Moore handed her his contacts, then said, "I'd like to talk to your friend Scarlet."

"I'll let her know."

Bob Moore and his partner were downstairs in their unmarked car bugging about the "terrorist attack in Harlem" when Five slid out the closet and said, "Good job, mama." His whole face was mangled, as he had suffered major injuries.

Maliah didn't even recognize her own son, and the truth of the matter was he was suffering from blunt trauma to the head. His conditions were worsening by the minute too. For the first time in her life Maliah was worried for her child. He looked like a monster.

"What really happened?"

"The niggas took my money," he grunted.

"How much ?"

"Everything. And it wasn't just my money."

"Who?"

"Stink..." Maliah yelped.

"Mama. They took my dad out the ground, and had him sitting in my car."

He couldn't even see out his eyes now. They were black and closed shut. He didn't know pain like that existed.

Maliah's hand covered her mouth. Her son's head had doubled in size, and there was no flesh on his face. On top of that, she knew Stink. In her eyes, Stink was friends with the devil. The world was at his feet, and that didn't just happen by the grace of God. He'd survived droughts, avoided the jail cell, escaped death. She was one of those conspiracy theorists, and always wondered how Capri went to jail but he didn't.

"Baby, he's a real gangsta. Cut your losses. They dug your daddy up to send you a message. Tried to blow you up. He probably sent those cops here," she panicked.

Five didn't need to hear that. He knew what he was up against, and was scared to death. He'd watched his boys leave him for dead, wanting no parts of this shit. They didn't even help him to safety. Karma, he thought fading out.

CHAPTER TWELVE

There Iris was again ruminating about a new life outside of New York, away from the miscreants and madness of the metropolis. Maybe Atlanta or Florida. North Carolina wasn't far enough away.

Atlanta was becoming the Black Hollywood. And who could resist good weather and the endless beaches of Miami -- which also held history for her. It's where she lost her virginity. She only had these thoughts when she was with her family, or when visiting Capri. On those trips up to the penitentiary she could forget her whole lifestyle. Everything! The line of work, her bi-curious behavior which was looking more like confirmation than inquisitive nature these days. But her parents, they could make her remember anything. Especially the change in her. All they had to do was mention the people next door, the mysterious Outens, before they appeared on the front page of every newspaper in the city.

Katrina Outen was once her bestie, and the host of her coming out party, but her death had very little impact, if any, on Iris. Katrina was just one less bitch she had to worry about vying for her man's attention. Before siding with the faction, Iris had only read about, or seen in films, the things they were doing. The sex, the drugs, the violence -- all of which she quickly adopted as her own.

A smirk slid across her shiny lips as she thought of the long gone BFF. This particular reflection had her back at that cheap crevice of a motel in the Carol City section of the M-I-A.

Eighteen again.

Innocent and chaste.

Open to anything, exposed to everything.

Iris stirred in her car seat as she recalled Capri performing a ferocious attack on her, remembered the six-foot gangsta pulling his engorged penis from her back door, then shoving it into Katrina's mouth, and moved in and out, before spewing all over Katrina's face and fresh doobie wrap. But it was the fact that his dick had gone from her ass to Katrina's mouth that excited her. Either of her lustful counterparts saw the smirk on her face that fervent night, nor could either imagine how special she felt watching Katrina be degraded. Up until that trip south, Iris had always thought the two were relatives, never expecting them to be in a wicked threesome that involved coke and commands, or to last three days. The raunchiest porn had nothing on this, and Iris relished it. Maybe Capri's viciousness had took up residence in her soul. He had never been in a movie, or won any awards, but to her he was a star.

Right before his 1996 arrest they'd popped bottles, got smoked out, and talked about everything while fucking and sucking the life out of each other. There was a closeness between the two, while Katrina and Action's murders bothered her the least. They fucked all night, and she loved it, while wondering had their trip to Miami been the cause. It wasn't confirmed, wasn't even mentioned, yet it aided in her climaxes, and she knew deep down there was no coincidence. Was she walking that thin line of a sociopath way back then?

The time and space that had come between the two was closing, and Iris couldn't wait to rejoice in Capri's sexual exploits, enact the insatiable thoughts he relayed in his letters, the naughtiness he brought with him every time they convened. Her G, the only dude she'd ever been with. And she could give two shits about his imbalance and unpredictability! There was nothing she wouldn't do for homie.

"...yo, I'm not gonna be able to make it," Iris hears after being on hold for several minutes. That wasn't what she wanted to hear.It was time to rock and roll. Everything was set. Just the way they'd planned it.

"Why, what's up? I don't understand."

Silence.

Iris said, "Dave, I'm not wearing any panties."

And then there it was –

"... yo, my right hand man is on life support. Got clapped a few days ago on a humble, and he might not make it. Shit is twisted right now."

"You just can't prepare yourself for stuff like this."

"And then, my girl calls me a few minutes ago talking about two detectives came to the club she works at."

This was perfect. Scarface Dave's world was collapsing right around him. His girl had problems with the law, his crime partner was hooked up to a respirator, and he sounded as fragile as a broken hearted bitch. Iris didn't want to push too hard, but what was too hard? He was responsible for some of the unthinkable, wasn't he? It was time to pay, wasn't it?

"You should let me take your mind off things. Put you at ease. Let me do that for you."

Dave hesitated, almost felt disloyal, but things were mounting and he did need some release. Even thought that maybe this was where he could start all over, leave his past behind if that's what things called for.

"Aiight, meet me on Jerome, by the Major Deegan Expressway."

"Right now?" Iris had placed just enough excitement in her undertone, laying the part of a eager damsel to the T.

Possessing that disarming charm Sunshine from Harlem Nights owned.

He replied, "Yeah, we'll go get a grub, and a room. I ain't eat all fuckin' day."

"Okay, cool," she replied, real giddily.

$ $ $

Jerome Avenue was teeming with used car lots, repair garages, and insurance companies. Above was the elevated train line, home of the number 4 train. And right in the midst of all these urban fixtures was the Major Deegan Expressway, also known as Interstate 87. Dave was just a few blocks away at Bronx Lebanon Hospital. Iris hadn't earned his complete trust, but at the same time, he didn't believe disaster could strike again in such close proximity of time.

Iris inhaled as she watched his set of wheels spin the busy corner of 174th Street with a nickel gleam that looked pretty in the darkness of the night. It was that type of light that had first blinded the college drop out in the first place. Only it wasn't in the Bronx by the West 174th Street underpass, it was in Harlem at a basketball tournament on Lenox Ave. With the flick of the wrist her highbeams blinked catching Dave's eye and his truck pulled up alongside her parked car. His eyes were puffy and he was forcing a smile. Someone else was driving though; his pupils were dilated and he never even looked Iris's way, just shot up a piece sign as he wheeled off leaving Dave on the curbside.

Just as quick as he opened her car door, Dave was sitting inside and shutting it. Iris forced a smile of her own as he took his jacket off. She was about to say it was too hot out for jackets, but then thought better when she located the straps to his shoulder holster hugging his upper body. He was packing two pieces, blue steel on either side. Both had a brand new look.

"I ain't ready to die," Dave professed adjusting the seat to accommodate his long legs. "Fuck that. All the shit we got away with, it could be anybody behind this shit."

"What about the cops visiting your soon-to-be ex-girl?
That have anything to do with --?"

"Her fucking nephew or some shit, something with his car.
Said it was Major Crimes."

"And you feel how about that?"

"She'll be aiight. She didn't do anything. I think. But ain't no telling what I might do to a nigga right about now. I don't know if you know, but me and my man, we goons for real.

But, how would you know?" There was a sharpness to his voice, and he was sitting upright when he said that. Iris pulled off with little doubt lingering, still feeling good about things.

Maybe the drama had heightened his senses instead of dulled them. Iris had one of those moments, the ones where a person's life flashed before their eyes. Still, she proceeded.

"What do you want to eat? And is there a hotel in particular you'd like for me to sit on that dick in, and ride it until that dick throw up? Bet you wanna spit that nut on my titties too, don't you? Or my face, huh? Oh, you one of those butt mans; I ain't forget you asked me if I like it in my ass, Negro."

Sex and guile! It was one of Iris's toxic combinations, sure to intoxicate a man. She whipped her hair back and waited for his answer.

"Jersey, where nobody knows us."

"New Jerus' it is then."

Iris took the Deegan to the George Washington Bridge, Lyfe Jennings CD playing at a soft tone. She was back to thinking about her future, then Dave began talking again. Obviously he was thinking about his future too, because he started telling Iris about his kid, his crew, his corners. Nothing she didn't already know. They did their homework. He started shooting theories out there about what he thought transpired with his homie, and who might be responsible. She didn't know much about Lava, but he had a death wish too. By the time they entered the Garden State, things she had no business knowing she now knew. The marathon his mouth was running made the cockpit of the Corvette feel more like a confessional, turning her off. That wasn't in the program. But she smiled, even caressed his crotch lightly with her fingertips until he became aroused. Took advantage of that too. Wasn't everyday she got to feel on a stiff dick.

They checked into a less than stellar spot Dave had given her direction to. Iris wasn't surprised he chose takeout over a table. She looked just that tasty that night in her flirty dress and wedge heels. She needed more time to think though, more time to ponder, to prepare, to execute. But there was no time. They were out back of a drive up that could really use some business. With their cartons of Chinese food and alcoholic beverages the two ducked into the room like they were stars and paparazzi was trying to get their picture. Behind the quickly closed door, Dave pulled Iris to him as soon as she sat their sustenance down. Forced his tongue inside her mouth. He held her with lust and power, his tongue moving feverishly. He breathed rather hard, savoring her. She could feel his bulge beginning to rise again. That's when her love and loyalty for her dude began to engineer rejection, deflect Dave's desires. He groaned like a wild man while holding onto her backside, half his hand wedged in the crack of her ass. And subconsciously she reached for his thickening dick and area of life Dave wasn't lacking in. It was right there against Iris's six pack and ribcage, elevating her sexual urges. In response, he squeezed her ass cheek before disarming himself. He had a devilish smirk on his face. And briefly, if only for a sec', she conveniently ignored the fact that he was the enemy, that a hundred grand had been electronically wired to her account for this job, as she was now living on the edge of sexual madness. She temporarily imagined his tongue on her inner thighs, his breath on her clitoris.

Iris felt climatic, vulnerable, like a traitor.

And Dave, he felt her heating up, and his problems fading fast. No one knew where they were, and it became too much goodness for Iris not to partake.

She felt the straps on her dress slip from her shoulders and Dave's tongue leave her vagina to meet her nipples. Her garment fell to the floor and her temperature shot through the roof. Dave sucked hard and passionately, like a seasoned lover on his second honeymoon. He grabbed hold of her thigh, lifted her left leg, held it close to him, told her, "I'm fuck the blood out of your li'l pretty ass. Yeah! I just don't know where first. And you're gonna enjoy it."

A glistening coat of perspiration had formed all over Iris's flesh. She told Dave, "Okay. But only with a condom."

"I hope you got one, because I don't," he returned with this tone in his voice that harbored very little cool. To the average woman it could've been scary even. Iris wasn't the average though.

She said, "A whole box. Think that'll be enough for what you got planned?"

"If it ain't, oh well. Just hurry the fuck up."

Before heading for her purse she released his erection and leered at him, made her lips curl up into a smile like she wanted to suck a nut out of it, then urged him not to move, demanded he stay put.

Dave kissed her again, his tongue deep, so deep that she'd know he liked kissing her pretty mouth. Iris kissed him back, then hit a sexy gait that he watched intently. His lady Scarlet had the meanest body he'd ever came across, but Iris could hold her head high if standing next to her. There was a slight bounce to her butt and breasts that made Dave salivate. He stepped out of his cargos and began stroking himself a bit, priming for the pounding. The last thing he wanted was to ejaculate prematurely.

Iris was moving quick, but her purse felt like a department store. She couldn't locate what she was looking for. There were condoms, mints, perfume, gum, lip gloss, keys, license, a few grams of caine. There it was, something she had been skeptical about since it was passed off. They called it secobarbital sodium, a liquid the color of iced tea with special effects. The syringe it was contained in was surgical and smaller than usual, so small it was undetectable.

Dave whacked away, his eyes on her. He saw her vacuum a white line up her left nostril, then the right. She had to be numb for this, just in case things went wrong. "I want him alive," replayed in her mind. Strict orders. Dave was to be alive. When the contract first came across her table, she questioned the plan and its designer. Iris was prone to squeezing triggers, with a specialty for getting close to her targets. People had collected life insurance off her work, got

rid of competitors, or just got even. But never had she made the kind of money this mission rewarded, and it didn't demand accuracy or a getaway plan. The coke took immediate affect, and Iris was prepared for the best.

While rolling a rubber onto Dave's rock hard penis, she fingered his shaft and balls, until she located the largest vein she could find. And then wham! It was there that she stabbed Dave sending him into a frenzy. Quickly, she curled up in a fetal position as he lashed out with blind fury. The sedative was supposed to put him on his ass for at least twelve hours, but it didn't seem to be working. Iris scampered towards the bed where a sharp shank was hidden in her shoe, prepared to give the cut on Dave's face some company. Maybe even put one on his throat; Dave's body temperature rose as he charged, arms flailing, screaming out in agony. Iris rose to her feet, blade in hand. But he finally got sluggish, weary, limp then fell face first on the tattered rug, right before Iris's bare feet. Impotent, he just stared up at her.

She knelt down, her bald pussy just inches from his face and sang, "You will never stick your dick in me, dickhead!"

$ $ $

The softness of Iris's voice was far more threatening than any shout Scarface Dave had ever heard. She was still naked when he came to, only wearing shoes, and fingering a half full champagne glass. Even from where he was tied down, imminent danger lingering heavily, her beauty was undeniable to him. And not just because it would be one of the odysseys he'd ever see. His fortune had changed. And he had very little idea what was in store for him.

Only six hours had passed a testament to his will. He was supposed to go under for twelve hours, according to Stink, whom she'd been awaiting for several hours. Right before she finally heard the knock at the door, she was saying something like, "I would have loved to shoot you, in broad day, with some big shit. That's what I wanted to do the day I first met you. It had taken me weeks to get that close to you.

"Once I was almost as close. You were barking on that faggot who drives you around. Yeah, he's into men," Iris said laughing. "I be knowing. And you are into him. What, women aren't enough? Y'all downlow ass niggahs gotta be all at the frank stand too?

"Yeah, you!" she barked.

There was that knock again. A light knock. Iris back peddled, eyes on Dave, shaking her head. She peaked out, then shot her orbs back at Dave. Like a sly fox, she pressed her back up against the door and creaked it open. In slid Stink.

He had always wanted to poke a nigga up. Shank a cat's face.

Always wondered what it was like to walk a prison yard. Wondered what a cell felt like once that door slammed shut at night. What goes through a nigga's mind, how he maintains his sanity under such conditions.

He thought of his homies and how things were structured behind the wall. The pow wows, the roll call, when it was time for war. How niggas really got their spots on the world wide lineup. What it would be like to see the entire Council convene at one time. Those brothers who were on the front line, scars all over their bodies from gang battles, or tens of years in the hole for standing for something redder than the dirt at a slaughter house. The ones who paved the way.

It was a twisted fantasy Stink lavished since the first time he heard a jailhouse story. Nah, not a story, more like an anecdote. It was almost like the kid was schooling Stink. And it wasn't just the drama, it was the parts that are less glamorized by homecoming gangstas. Mail droughts that last for months. Disconnected phone numbers. When the soft vibe of a feminine voice that only a chick can deliver no longer caresses the ears. Dude told Stink he'd seen a few cats crumble to the point that they thought it was cool to be with anybody, long as it ain't a dead body.

Maybe that's what kept Stink so sharp, undetectable to police, so discreet about his larceny. Maybe that's why he may never know what the inside of a cell is like, what pops off in prison yards. But, he was about to see what it felt like to put work in without a gun!"

Stink gave Iris the once over, then found a chair a few feet from the table. There was two lines left behind. Stink sat, started removing items from his pockets.

109

Iris sat back and watched Stink. It   was   like   she   was watching someone she didn't really know. Stink had a Colgate toothbrush in his hand with a razor melted to the tip.On the table where he was just sitting was a piece of steel that had been modified to resemble a dagger. It was sharp, very very sharp! And shiny.

Iris also noticed that Stink was wearing some starched green slacks, crisp construction Timbs, and a mean button down shirt made by her favorite designer. He looked just like one of the homies in those flicks of Capri and his boys, Iris had been receiving for years.

As she started getting dressed Iris watched intently, heard Stink shout, "What's poppin, bee?" He was pacing, his limp ever so visible. The anger was evident too. "You already know what pop though, you just didn't respect it."

This wasn't the calculated dude Iris watched take vows, hustled with for years, respected as much as she did Capri and Zest, the philanthropist working to bring awareness to the ineffective assistance of counsel crisis.

Her dress was adorning her body again by the time Stink looked her way again. He said, "Get out of here. Take the whip I pulled up in, the keys are still in it and something else for you. Leave the keys to the Corvette. I'll get rid of it when I'm done with this twirp."

Dave was still groggy, his throat and insides arid dry. He was tied down, gagged, his eyes bouncing back and forth like a ping pong ball in a heated game of table tennis. The epitome of fear.

To her own surprise, Iris did as she was told. Got out of there.

When she got in the Dodge Magnum, she noticed a bonus in

the passenger seat. Iris flicked through the knot almost as thick as her thigh. All big face Benjis. Iris looked back, pursed her lips, then shifted into first. There was a left turn, then a straight away, the GW Bridge just a few miles ahead. The first thing she did when she got back to the city was shower. She had to get Dave's scent off her. She then looked in the mirror, imagined what her face would look like had Dave's haymaker connected before roaming naked, wishing it wasn't so late, then maybe Pri could call from jail. She needed someone to talk to. About anything that would divert her thoughts from the scene she'd just left.

She found herself thinking about Dave's girl and what might she'd gotten herself into. Major Crimes meant just that: Major crimes. She thought she was the only bitch in the city getting paid like a man to do a man's work.

After a glass of white wine she started flicking through the cable stations. Her intent was to watch some porn, masturbate and mellow out, not helplessly await a call from Stink telling her everything was all good.

Upon her invasion of cable TV, she found a scene of a white girl favoring Friends' star Jennifer Aniston having her asshole reamed. It was actually a parody of the hit show. She watched for a sec, then hit the up arrow on the remote, just surfing. Channel One's late night news was airing a recap just as she passed. She quickly turned back. The reporter, a brown skinned brother, mentioned a car bombing not far from the Harlem River Drive, and Iris immediately thought of Dave's girl, not the Al Qaeda connection they were tossing around. She then thought of Five, noticing a set of rims behind the reporter only he was riding on. She was there when Stink had him tossed out of the Ruby Red, and made a mental note to let Stink know that if that was his work, that the body found in the BMW wasn't Five's. Iris happened to date a girl a while back who had it bad for Five. He would tell the girl all his business, and based on what the girl had shared with Iris, he could be a problem.

The next segment was about a shooting. Iris listened for a while, then changed channels. Iris thought of Scarface Dave, and then his girl again. Then there was the comrade Dave'd left back at the hospital to walk into her trap.

Iris dozed off grinning. The remnants of the snicker was still on her face when she woke up the next morning to no words from Stink, the crime boss.

CHAPTER THIRTEEN

The large "CASA MARIE" sign fronting Mrs. Pierce's home away from home could be seen from blocks away. And it brought life to the 3400 block of the Grand Concourse. Restaurant reviewers had been quoted as saying "too trendy for neighborhood." But Rosa couldn't have thought better of the location if God asked. Each day all the unsold food went to the residents living in the building above the trending eatery. And on weekends she had a "Balling On A Budget" menu that received no reviews, but made her heart smile and gave the less fortunate a taste of the good life.

That morning Rosa rose from bed in this teal blue teddy Stink had picked out for her on Rodeo Drive earlier that year. Or was it during the 2003 East Coast Blackout when they were in Los Angeles to see Dave Chapelle live at the House of Blues? Rosa wasn't sure. Nor was she sure about the time of Stink's departure the night before.

Stink had rolled out of bed and left their property in a quick gait. Rosa was thinking about their life at the time, and whether or not she could continue the way they were living. If it were up to her they'd just go back to the way things used to be. The good ole days. Hanging out on 115th Street. Catching movies on 86th and Broadway. Sharing hotdogs at Papaya World. Just talking about the simplest stuff. She would forgive and forget. She was prepared to do that, put it all behind them. There was nothing beneath the teal blue teddy, just glistening flesh scented with Chanel No. 9. She wanted to make up, make her argument, then stake her claim. But Stink had jetted and hadn't returned.

There it was! The huge sign baring Rosa's middle name. Two blocks away. One block away from where she'd lived until the age of thirteen. Her humble beginnings. Rosa's household was very dysfunctional as a youth, filed with turmoil. Her comfort came from preparing meals for her younger sisters, and getting stellar grades in school. That was her father's fault. He reminded her of Ricky Ricardo, suave and rugged at the same time. Around the time of her tenth birthday and she realized he was a big flirt, though she didn't know he was sleeping with several women in their neighborhood, and a few in their building.

Instead of approaching the situation, confronting him, Rosa's mother ran off. Rosa cried when her mother moved the family to the other side of the Bronx. She was able to bilk him out of half the small fortune he'd accumulated since illegally entering the country.

In ways, Rosa felt just like her mother, except there were no children involved. She knew Stink was a cheater, and was too afraid to confront him.

She remembered when it started. She recalled wanting to contact CHEATERS, but quickly abandoned the idea. Stink would never take kindly to being tailed by private investigators, so Rosa did it herself. Followed him for hours one day, days one week, until her worse fears were finally confirmed.

They were holding hands, and doing this new thing called canoodling. Stink had let the girl's hand go in exchange forth palming of her basketball shaped butt cheek. The girl was amazingly attractive, her hair whipping around her face, and her curves snapping the necks of the watchful men casting appreciative glances at Stink's arm candy.

Not only was Rosa heart broken, but she went on to experience countless headaches of epic proportions. She considered divorce, flirted with counseling -- but that meant approaching Stink, confrontation and conclusion. And he had a way about him that even scared her at times. No confrontation. So instead she played it like nothing was happening, although all the passion he possessed and showered her with now belonged to another woman. And, the many mistresses she went on to find out were accompanying Stink on many of those business trips, that turned out wasn't always business. The newlyweds, and once best friends, had gone from fucking twice, sometimes three times a day, to once in a blue. The spontaneity was gone, obsolete like outdated Microsoft, or washed up vets. Their intimate moments, the kind married couples cherish, had become planned, sometimes weeks in advance.

On one of those planned getaways Rosa had packed a business plan she'd been working on, just so they would have something to talk about other than his endeavors which were doubling and tripling by the day. More reason for him to be away. The well written and thought out proposal was for Casa Marie. It was her attempt to not only prove her independence, but increase her importance as well. Who wants to be minimized after experiencing multitudes of love from someone they admire beyond belief?

The two were sprawled out on beach chairs and sands alongside the astonishingly clear azure waters of Cabo San Lucas, at the tip of the Beja California peninsula. Stink took his shades off, uncrossed his ankles, and with what was more like a gander looked over her presentation. He was immediately drawn in and suggested he finance the project. He looked her in the eye, told her he loved her idea, the creativity and the originality. Just to hear love come out his mouth did more for Rosa than the sun kissing her skin could ever do for the entire world.   He   wasted no time giving her the backing she needed in the form of a blank check, and adamantly expressed he expected nothing in return. She celebrated by secretly forgiving Stink's indiscretions, only to be slighted as soon as they had returned to New York with a girl named Scarlet.

This time she wasn't going to cry herself to sleep, she wasn't going to eat herself into ten pounds of dreaded weight gain, she wasn't going to pray about it. Rosa got Stink back.

Like Diane Lane, she became the object of pleasure in a bathroom stall, risky and risqué, and tittered shamelessly about it on the way home! That's what happens when you believe your lover has lost faith in devotion.

The restaurant was only half full, and all the patrons were trying to play it half-ass cool. This was the Boogie Down, and it was the land of the umber cool. It wasn't the internationally diverse crowd Rosa'd hoped to some day channel, but it was a good looking group of natives. Most of them had their own things going on, but none could help but steal a glimpse of the owner entering with her sensuous full lips, flowing platinum hair, just dyed the day before, and the suddenly lit he figure of the goddess of vengeance.

Rosa moved freely in her flowing dress and open toes, greeting the patrons one at a time, before grinning with some of the people who were so important in the formative stages of her new career. Then she spotted some beckoning eyes that belonged to a guy sitting alone, chomping at a salad and sipping an extra-large mojito. The top two buttons on his shirt was open, and she could see the hair on his scalped chest which was dark and rich like the beard bringing the rugged character to his face. He could never replace Stink in Rosa's heart, but he had a slight advantage when it came to her body. He'd been doing things to her that just drove her bananas, things that she wished she could brag to someone about. Seventh Heaven! Senses she had no idea even existed were awakened, flowing orgasms that lasted for minutes.

With a lot of Stink's qualities, it was easy for Rosa to get caught up with this younger guy. But those kisses down low to her were like the blood of Jesus to an evangelist.

"Who're you wearing?" he asked like he was some savvy red carpet correspondent tapping into the reservoir of a fashionista.

"Cavalli."

"The shoes?"

"Jimmy Choo."

"So, how'd it go?" he rushed out, trading his fork for the neck on his drink. "I couldn't help but think that I may never see you again the way I've been able to for the last month."

"Things went well," Rosa lied. She wanted to see how he would react. "I, just, may be able to save my marriage."

117

CHAPTER FOURTEEN

It was Iris's first time inside the Statue of Liberty, and she had never felt more liberated. It was a time of reflection, evolution, celestial peace. She'd just grabbed a bite alone at one of East Village's quaint little staples before leaving the city by ferry. There was no coke in her bag, or a desire for the vice. The gig with Stink presented a payday that had put Iris's net worth at a little over $400K, five times what she'd been projected to gross three years removed from college, which would've been right around now had she not been derailed, as her morn liked to put it. She thought about the horrid surroundings she chose, leaving behind her uppercrest chum of Queens, and cringed a little. While she worked in collusion with some depraved entities for the last eight years, with the exception of the slain Katrina Outen, all of her friends were now either cultivating careers or nurturing families. Iris would be thirty in a few years, and time wasn't slowing down for her. There were a lot of things missing in her life.

As she embraced her peace, the cool air of the waters below traveled with the light winds caressing her face. She took her shades off and peered nowhere in particular. Being an only child came to mind as it did many times. A circumstance that engineered a strong imagination and a heavy dose of daydreaming. While her parents always assumed she'd master something that would lead to a Masters in something, she was daydreaming about gangstas and goons and the girls they gallivanted with. If there was going to be a story about Iris, she was going to tell it.

No one knew exactly how much was raging beneath Iris's surface, not even the man she gave so much of herself to and for. The kind of power she'd hoped to receive from Capri was in the hands of another woman. At times she even felt like an afterthought, a casualty in his war against Action, and then there were days she'd fall asleep with remnants of his affection on her taste buds. It was no secret she wanted to be more than just some sparkling ingénue he could fuck with when he wanted to. Even he knew it. The onus was on Iris to make that happen, to be vigilant about her feelings and future.

There was someone who existed with thoughts of Iris as high as the fortress she was standing in. A multicultural cornerback on a mediocre NFL team. Nowhere near as mesmerizing as Capri, but physically fit and educated and would probably give anything for a piece of Iris.

Her phone buzzed, and "What a surprise" escaped her.

"Yo, I want you to come to my premiere party to check out the trailer for my first adult film. The principle actress gonna be there, and you just might like what you see. Her name's Bananas. And -- her body is bananas!"

Iris scoffed. That was a part of her life she really wanted to delete. How could she ever be taken serious as a lover if she allowed her affinity for girls to thrive? She wanted desperately to be spoken for, madly adored -- more than anything.

Zest didn't know that. He didn't think he was encouraging her to cheat on Capri by saying that. It was Capri's fault, being so cagey when it came to his thing for Iris.

"No, I can't make it!'

Zest sensed the contempt, said, "Yo, what up???"

"Things have to change. That's all."

"What are you talking about?"

"I'm not just some side chick, a jump off, and you shouldn't be encouraging me to be promiscuous like I am, when you know how I fuck with your cousin. My proclivities should make you look at me like I'm being disloyal, you shouldn't be setting me up, Zest."

"Damn, my bad. I didn't know it was like that. I just thought..."

"What did you think?"

"That it was more of a fixation than some forever shit."

"He was my fucking first! I spent a month and a half fucking him every day before he went to jail! I went to see him once a month for eight years since he's been in jail. I am who I am because of him..." Iris wept. That day she was decked out in Cavalli from head to toe, so there were eyes on her. Even a few ears twitched.

"My bad, yo. You acting like I just blew your car up in the middle of Harlem of something."

"Did you just say, like you blew a car up in the middle of Harlem?" she whispered, her eyes darting around.

"Saw the news," Zest said laughing.

"That dude is not dead."

"What dude?" Zest played stupid, though surprised.

"You know what dude."

"How you know?"

120

"I watch the news."

"You coming or what?" asked Zest trying not to think too hard.

"You'll be staying with me."

"What made you get into porn anyway? Like, who goes from a street general to making pornos?" Before Zest could answer, Iris added, "What, you staring in it too?"

Even Zest had to laugh at that, the thought having crossed his mind one time, or ten. "Iris we gotta have an exit. See what Stink's doing, right? That nonprofit shit is gonna bring him in way more money than he put out. Don't get me wrong, it's gonna do a historically deprived race some good, but it'll also create other opportunities. I'm really trying to get into film period, and this is a fast track plan. Right before I left for New York the other day --"

"You were in New York the other day, when?"

"-- I was partying with this Russian kid, his pops got parts of some alcoholic beverage coming out of Monaca. And then this other cat, he bringing girls straight over from Brazil. Pussy that never even been fucked on camera over here before, never worked in a film studio. And, that Brazilian pussy cost like snowflakes on the Hill in Harlem!"

"And what is the name of this porno?"

"Brazilian Butt Loving!"

"Anal sex?" Iris queried. "I heard you love anal..."

"Really?" Iris sulked, second guessing everything in her life.

"You know Capri is my first cousin, and we used to talk."

So much for her liberation. "That is not cool, Zest. I don't care how fuckin' close you two are."

"Come on, ma. It ain't even like that."

"Whatever. I bet he don't talk about Christine like that," Iris lamented. "Bet he never did Patience like that? Why vocalize my sexual exploits?! Fuck!"

A cool breeze soaring off the river sent a chill up the nape of Iris's neck. She shivered, stretched and yawned, before reclaiming the sultry posture her heels gave her. "I want Capri to come home and change. This can't be life."

"What do you mean?"

"I want him to come home... to me, move away from here ... with me, just travel the world for a while... with me."

"You know he's gonna want to be where his kid is," Zest responded. "And Christine don't let that little girl out of her sight. Need I say more?"

"What if he had another baby?" asked Iris. "What if..."

"Yo, Iris I fucks with you and all that, but I got other invites to get out, so I can't entertain the causes and affects of y'all shit."

Iris felt like Janet Jackson probably did in wake of Super Bowl XXXVIII's "Nipplegate" incident. Betrayed, misunderstood, and full of rage. "Congrats on your business move. Maybe I need to reevaluate my goals and aspirations."

"The party's in two weeks, in case you change your mind."

"Pri comes home in about two weeks," Iris chimed, instead of vilifying Capri for misplacing her trust.

"Yeah, he'll be on deck."

"Okay, I have your number. Be safe."

Iris ended the call with a discerning smirk. She took one last look from her vantage point, took in a couple compliments from some watching men of foreign decent, then descended the stairs. "I need to get extreme about my beliefs like y'all muthafuckers," she said in this hushed tone.

On the ferry ride back into the city, Iris wept, a controlled release that went pretty much unnoticed on the commute. It baffled her that someone she thought so much of, thought so little of her. Reality struck! She was nowhere near the calculating woman who hardly smiled she often stared down in her mirror. She was failing miserably in her personal life.

Inside her car, she finally got a call from Stink.

"About time, nigga! Had me all worried and shit."

"I can finally get on with my life. Thanks, word up ma."

Iris thought he sounded so sweet, that his words were saturated with sincerity, something she'd been getting very little of. "You're welcome. Tell Rosa I said hi, and I'll see you soon."

"I'll do that. Can't wait to see her. I really miss my wife."

"You sound like you haven't seen her in a while, like y'all don't share the same bed."

Stink didn't respond swift enough for Iris's liking, so she asked, "YO, what's really good? That cheating done caught up with you?"

"There's never a storm before the calm, yo." There was a moment of silence. "I'm not the only one having extramarital affairs."

CHAPTER FIFTEEN

"Vroom-vroom-vroom!" was the sound of the engine as Stink hit the gas pedal before shifting into first. He was in route to the GW Bridge and into the city. The timekeeper on his wrist read 3:20. He had exactly an hour and forty minutes to spare.

Phil Collins' classic and widely accepted in urban communities hit "I Can Feel It in The Air," played at a relaxing tone immersing Stink in the drowning drums as he handled his crimson 600 Benz coupe through Route 46 rearing the toll booths.

Thoughts of Rosa entered his mind as he flashed the latina in the booth his easy-pass. When he left their manse the other night, he'd also left behind a glint in her eye he hadn't seen in a long time. Her recent weight loss made her undeniable. And he couldn't help but think of the sexy teddy she was in, or the new blonde do. It was the one time he didn't have thoughts of divorce when he eyed her. And couldn't control the urge to ravish her. And he was certain that's exactly what she wanted. She had an up-rise in the corners of her mouth and a sturdiness in her nipples. It looked like so much was going on in her mind that night.

Once in the city he hit a storage den and purchased a box of $300 Nicaraguan cigars, a cutter and a new lighter that ran thirty

124

bucks. Peanuts to a player of his magnitude.

Shandy had set up a visit to Hot 97 for him, amongst some other events she planned to attend with him. It was crunch time, but he had to make one stop first.

Back behind the wheel, Stink sped through Midtown, slowing up to a respectable limit when he crossed 110th Street. He looked to his right, the beginning of Central Park was there, a spot his father would take him when he was a young lad. He passed his old block, his old hood, getting the love he almost felt like he lived for at times. He noticed a young hottie, early twenties he'd been trying to smash for a couple weeks. She was scantily clad, standing on stilettos, looking the part of a home wrecker.

Not even she could believe Stink kept going, left her stargazing on the corner of 116th and 7th Avenue.

It was one of several moves towards getting his life back in order. His mental, his physical, his spiritual.

His pops wanted him to convert to Islam, but Stink was already a standing member of a 20,000 seat Harlem sanctuary with a congregation of 8,000, led by a charismatic and flashy fellow known as Pastor P. Political pundits wanted the 30-year old Jada Kiss lookalike investigated for fraud and possible misuse of church-owned assets. But he was walking easy, standing tall, delivering his sermons of perseverance, while serving as a spiritual advisor to guys like Stink. It was really his slang and his swag, the very thing the community identified with, that his haters disliked.

Stink was just a block from the church, which is where he was headed. He wanted to discuss the infidelity in his union. The young pastor let Stink vent first, absorbed what he needed.

"How did it start?" was the first thing Pastor P asked. "You

125

know I come from the mud, bee."

"We come from the same place, bro. Same upbringings.

I'm from the mud," he said, loosening the bright red tie around his neck.

"Okay, well around 1996, I took a lot of loses. Friends, family, my stride when I was shot. I couldn't play ball anymore, which was one of my primary releases, I couldn't kick it with my skrap Capri no more because he was in jail, so I sought relief in other places. Those places were other women.

"The same year I got married, I started seeing other chicks, staying out, partying, strip clubs, private parties, all the seedy shit that soils your commitment. In the last four years I've slept with about a thousand different women from all walks of life. Safe sex, but --"

"Has your wife ever confronted you on your infidelity?"

Stink looked at his diamond band, the ring Rosa had put on his hand. "Nah."

"So she doesn't know?"

"I mean, she has to know something. I love everything about women, every curve, every feminine thing, everything, she knows that, and I barely touch her now. So she gotta know?"

"Why wouldn't she address it then? I find that to be odd.

Have you ever approached her about her indiscretions?"

"No," Stink replied shaking his head.

"Do you have concrete evidence of her unfaithfulness?"

"When your chick goes from dark misery to a godly glow, and you're not dicking her down, you're not the giver of that light, there's gotta be someone else fulfilling her needs. So I know there's a dude, I just don't know who he is."

"Or who they are," Pastor P said to Stink's dislike. "If there

126

was more than one could you still forgive and forget as you expect her to?"

"I don't know, bee!"

"I've never heard anything like this," Pastor P admitted. "There has to be a lot of pinned up anger. Has to be. And a catastrophe is brewing, Stink. You do know that right?"

"With the exception of business and bills, I've pretty much been moving through a haze the last couple years.   I be there, but I don't. When I see her smiling some days I wanna ask her what the fucks she smiling about. When she doesn't come home, or suddenly feels the need to go away I wanna become the possessive nigga and take her car keys, but I know I'm doing wrong, so..."

"You have to be the x-factor and the catalyst in this mission if you truly want to save your marriage."

"Yeah, but I've created bonds with women that I don't love, but I do harbor feelings of affection for. There are emotional attachments."

Pastor P nodded, because he understood. A lot of power had been invested in him, a lot of women trusted him, and he in the past like many pastors, had misplaced that trust before realizing that he had a really great woman at home. "When you hear – a dedication to the integrity of love -- what comes to mind?"

"Can't really say."

"That's what marriage is, O.G. Stink!" Stink stared.

"There's a verse that always comes to mind when I'm approached about infidelities. Proverbs 5:19, '... may her breasts satisfy you always.'" He put a hand on Stink's right shoulder, stared him in the eyes, went, "It boils down to intimacy in marriage, loving the spousal bond you've created and share.

Being content, being satisfied, being faithful."

"I want to make things right with her. That's one of the most important things right now. The other night she looked so good, there was energy there, and then I got pulled away. "

"By another woman?"

"Yeah, not, I mean nah, on some business."

"What if she doesn't want to make things right with you? what if --"

They spoke a little more, the pastor led them in special prayer, then Stink was back on the road, cigar in mouth, thinking of the right words he could give everyone involved. Rosa, Shandy, and his lovely ingenue Azure.

$ $ $

"We got the homie Stink from One-hundred-and-fifteenth street in the building to discuss his nonprofit organization!" What's poppin', boy-boy?" the popular radio personality sounded off with a genuine gleam in his eyes.

"You know, on my gangsta mogul 'ish, trying to make my contribution to this revolution we started in 1993. Shout out to all the big homies on lock down behind the g-wall, all the big homies on keep lock, the ones who stuck, and the ones on they way out," replied Stink as he sat upright before a brand new microphone and a dozen watchful eyes that belonged to men and women.

"I've known you for a minute now, what about ten years?"

"Yeah, about that."

"You've always possessed a power and love and discipline that's not seen in most street cats. How did you achieve the balance, for the younger brothers out there who may look up to you that you don't know."

"A belief in a higher power, something greater than me and my abilities. That fifteen percent of spirituality."

"You were under some scrutiny a couple months ago for your upbringing, the culture we now see in the streets of New York. That being the gang culture. I saw a stream online of your launch for Accountability Where It Counts, and I think you handled yourself well."

"It almost got super ugly out there," Stink remembered.

"Yeah, but you held it down."

"See it wasn't about me, but you know how reporters are, these bloggers and hater get down. It was about guys like me in bad situations due to a lack of adequate legal representation. That's what my nonprofit is all about. The people, a historically deprived race, racial discrimination, and racial group oppression. Rest In Peace, George Jackson!"

There was a moment of silence in the studio for the long dead revolutionary most known for his association with the Black Panthers and his stellar literary offering, BLOOD IN MY EYE, who too was misrepresented in a court of law.

"So you have a real serious political conscience?"

"I study the history of Black people, and I'm overriding oppression and destruction. These people are trying to destroy our communities and break up our families by sending young black men away for long prison terms, which is just another form of slavery. Once you're convicted you can't vote, a felony puts brothers in a social caste that just makes life so much harder."

"Yo, this brother is deep!" the radio personality snapped.

"Jim Crow wanted us segregated fifty, sixty years ago, today they want to segregate us through the court system. If my foundation can change the way brothers get represented in those courtrooms, then I've succeeded in my mission."

"You did get married too, I know, because I covered the wedding when I was on my blogger grind and writing for the Ghetto Quran Magazine."

"Yeah, Rosa ... I married my best friend."

"Black love, son!" the radio personality mused. "Just in the last two years I been hearing brothers talking on that level, jumping the broom. You did it five years ago. A trendsetter for real."

Stink smiled.

"I know you've been doing some nice things on the up and up for a minute now, I mean it's every street cat's dream, I think, to go legit, right? Any advice?"

"Oh, for sure! Nobody wants to remain a rookie, nobody wants to just make the playoffs, nobody wants to continue being conference champions. Eventually you want to win it all, be at the pinnacle of success. Then you want to own things. And in order to do so, one must evolve, even reinvent himself, or herself. My advice, focus on course until satisfied!"

"With that said, what's your take on the bazaar rash of c rimes uptown?"

"Like what?"

"The car bombing on 155th? Removing dead bodies from gravesites? The rapes? And they just discovered a dude from the BX with his organs missing.

Son was heavy in the streets so like a lot of people, I was shocked to hear Scarface Dave had been discovered with his kidneys and heart missing."

A female with a pretty smile jumped on her mic, chimed in and said, "There's been a booming market for organs, but that's something that just never reached our demographic."

Stink nearly lost the color in his deep brown skin, as ashen as Casper the Friendly Ghost. Oh, but there was nothing friendly about what he did to Dave. His response was delayed.

"Well, um, this is definitely a new wave. As far as an opinion, I'll leave that up to the people who get paid to have those type of opinions. I'm here to discuss Accountability Where It Counts."

"So, before you leave us, let all the listeners know what else you got going on."

"Got the Auto Sound in Harlem, come through and get your systems and rims, alarms and all that. My wife got the restaurant on the Grand Concourse, Casa Marie, incredible latin cuisine with a twist of soul. And then there's the nonprofit organization, which is why I'm here. We're having a seminar next month, several law students will be on hand for advice and to answer legal questions. Experienced criminal lawyers will also be there giving out contact info for family members to pass to incarcerated folks looking to overturn wrongful convictions."

"Okay, we're gonna take some calls before you bounce. Line one, go ahead."

"Will the lawyers be willing to represent defendants probono or what?"

Stink said, "Appeal specialists will be taking on select cases, and not just DNA cases like these other innocent projects. Trial attorneys will be communicators, the filter between defendants and the lawyers who don't communicate with their clients. Next question."

131

"Caller two..."

"Yes, this is EvaNae, I'm from the Boogie Down. I'm try'na get a job at your strip club! Ass is fat, -bleep- is fat --"

"On more caller..."

"Hey, ummmh, where can I make a donation?"

"Accountability-where-it-counts-dot-org."

Stink went from Hot 97 to Power 105, from there to another speaking engagement where Shandy accompanied him. It was the first time they were together since their initial meeting and Stink didn't feel the need to touch Shandy. She didn't look too deep into it, and just embraced the man's evolution. The only time she'd seen Stink more focused was naked and alone with her in a hotel suite.

That night Stink did a 100 mph straight home, only slowing up for traffic lamps. He almost got pulled over, and was so in a rush, he left the car lights on as he scampered through the sliding glass door at the rear of his home.

The cherry red Bentley Continental Stink had given Rosa was in her parking spot. She had beat him home, and was listening to some kid named Mario's newest hit "Let Me Love You" as she looked over some financial statements from the restaurant. Stink embraced Rosa from behind and inhaled. "You smell good," he let out in a soft delicate tone that put her right at ease. The kind of ease only a husband could provide.

He eased his hands over her hips, her thighs, around to her pelvic, up across her midsection, slowing his range right where her breasts began. He squeezed and caressed, and Rosa exhaled, her body heating up with Stink's every touch. "Don't let me go, please," Rosa asked.

132

Neither spoke again. What was understood needed no explanation.

They had a late night and an early morning. Even had breakfast together for the first time in months. They showered together, made love again and again, then it was back to the business. Their laptops.

Stink had an e-mail from his PR about his approval rating, and thought they should celebrate the success. Stink e-mailed her back with the contacts for the few he wanted to attend.

Got it!..., she e-mailed back along with the restaurant's address and expected arrival time.

Rosa walked up and kissed Stink's ear, jaw, and the side of his neck, in that order and passionately. Kissing was the one thing she did keep sacred during her time of revenge.
Stink was logging on to the nonprofit website. The aid was pouring in. Almost $100,000 in donations.

Rosa said, "They believe in you, our people, they trust you Marcel. You talked about it, and you aid it. And this will only add to your brand. I'm eager to see what's next."

"Us, that's what next. Us."

"I like the sound of that. And, I like to think that it may be time for us to start being us again, the best us."

"You still want kids?" Stink asked looking Rosa square in her soft eyes.

Rosa smiled, ran her pretty fingernails through her golden mane, told Stink, "Only if you get me pregnant."

CHAPTER SIXTEEN

It was hot out, muggy, the sun was finally setting after a long day of shining. The sky had a redness to it that almost illuminated the darkening streets in an eerie way. The beverages, urine and everything else that had hit the pavement that day could be smelled in the thick air. The street lamps would be on any minute, give or take. Folks were all talking at once, no one could really hear the other, all meandering noisily. Where astonishing surprise existed in some, emotion was absent on others. This was a time when communities were supposed to come together, but Drew Hamilton Projects couldn't have been any more divided. And for some reason, the residents of this troubled neighborhood didn't seem the least surprised by the developing story, thought a blue collar cop, watching one female with a nonchalant attitude get ridiculed.

One of the first cops on the scene said, "An eight-year-old girl was snatched off the streets while under custodianship of her grandmother."

"How long has she been missing?" another officer asked.

"Said the last time she saw the little girl was around noon."

"Where's the grandmother now?" asked yet another officer.

"Right there, pulling hard on that cigarette."

There was nicotine smoke pluming from Mecca's nostrils and

mouth, this sedated gloss in her almond shaped eyes. She was holding her Newport tight, her free hand clinging to her elbow as she tried to contemplate what had gone terribly wrong. She had only turned her head for a brief moment. Or was it longer? She remembered a fem sauntering by, young with rich features. She recalled two guys zooming through on dirt bikes, two guys she had never seen.

"And who's in charge?" the first officer quizzed swiping beads of sweat from his upper lip.

"Major Crimes Unit."

Just as the brawny cop said that, Bob Moore and his partner dismounted their unmarked cruiser. Moore's workout had been interrupted for this case, hand picked by the Police Commissioner himself. He'da been thrilled had he not been following up on a lead that led him to the Bada Bing, a strip club in the Bronx, the night before. They had reason to believe that the girl who owned the car-bombed BMW was also the girlfriend of the guy who'd been mutilated and left for dead.   Topless beauties were all over the club, tip drills going down everywhere, no sign of Scarlet though. They were supposed to make another trip over there, hoping her life wasn't too in danger. But when Amber Alerts pop, all else goes to the wayside. Solving a case of this magnitude could mean big things for the seasoned crime solver. "All hell could break lose," Moore was told, by his supervisor, "if this little girl isn't found alive."

"A one way block, 143rd Street, looks like the first night of Harlem Week," sounded off Moore. "We can barely get through."

Moore followed up with, "What do we know so far?"

"Not much," replied the brawny officer. "The grand mother called it in, that's it."

"Could she be involved?"

"What does she have to gain?" Moore responded. From what he'd been told on his way over to the crime scene, the child's authority figures had no money troubles. In fact they were negro rich!

"Word is the little girl's Capri Hayward's kid," both Major Crimes detectives had l earned at the same time. They looked at each other. Capri had been the topic of much discussion within law enforcement circles. His upcoming release had not only been documented, but heavily monitored. The last time he was released from prison was the summer of 1996, and there were more than thirty murders that summer.

"Where's the grandmother?" asked Moore. Mecca stuck out like a sore thumb.

"She looks more aggravated than devastated," Moore couldn't help but notice.

"What's she supposed to look like with her grandchild missing?" Moore's partner reckoned.

"Good question..." said a cop who patrolled the area at least four days a week.

There were four male voices nursing the conversation, all four of them eyeing Mecca like she was a raw steak and they were pitbulls. For good reason. More flesh than cloth.

In 1997 she left her post at the hospital, a twenty grand a year gig she'd worked hard to acquire. Just 37 at the time, she went from being an effective mother with the affordable habits of two daughters, to the ghetto queen with a million dollars at her disposal. While Christine moved away, Mecca stayed in the projects trying to relive her youth thought some of her peers. The strong black woman Christine once admired had become this pretentious, self-absorbed winch Christine couldn't stand to be around. Often times Mecca resembled the mother of a hot mess on the seediest daytime talk show. The ones exploiting the worse in minorities, and designed to degrade a rising race. Now forty-five, life was even more of a party. She was sleeping with more women than some of the hustlers in the projects. The women she once sat, drank and smoked cigarettes with, had been relegated to jesters and bot bottom-feeders. Capri was Mecca's unofficial son-in-law, and the entire community was on notice.

Moore flexed his muscles, said, "Anybody could have walked away with this ghetto's princess."

This wasn't their perusal of favorite crime scenes. They certainly didn't expect to be lusting over the long legs sprouting from the metallic Christian Louboutin heels on Mecca's feet, or the lush breasts spilling out of her teal bustier.

Any shorter and her denim shorts would've been dungaree panties too small for her buttocks. Moore wondered had she gone under the knife for that body, then started giving out orders.

The cadre of cops eyeing Mecca began canvassing the scene again hoping to find a clue, or some nosy neighbor would come forward with something. Anything. They knew with each passing minute the chances of little Olivia returning home were diminishing. Moore kept a close eye on Mecca. It was almost as if she was in another world, absent minded. The only evidence of her consciousness was the smooth movement of the cigarette going to and from red lips.

The DT's took a gander of the photos Mecca had supplied of Olivia: kindergarten, cap and gown, second grade class photo, a family portrait, the little girl being held with her daddy.

One DT sighed and said, "These things never end good," in

sheer frustration.

"She's right here in Harlem, probably in these projects. I can feel it, Moore said looking up at the towering buildings erected in the early 1900's. "Hopefully no sicko has her--"

"Lord I hope not," countered his partner.

The two detectives were about to make their first contact with Mecca when a Mercedes lunch box, all black, on twenty inch rims, came roaring through, lurching to a halt. The driver's side door flung open and the circle of officers watched as a passenger jut forward screaming, "I know who got my fucking baby! How did you let this happen?!"

Moore inched his way between the two women before the younger of the two could assault the other. "Did you say you know who has your child?" he asked, unable to control his eyes.

Christine had no doubts about who'd taken little Olivia. No reservations about accusing the person. And could give two fucks what anyone thought. "Yes, I saw her loitering around my house a few times."

"Did she ever speak to your daughter?"

"Yes. She did."

"And what did this woman you saw talking to your daughter say to your daughter if you know?" Moore pressed.

"She told my daughter that she looked just like her father," Christine remembered.

"That the woman looked like your daughter's father?"

"No, stupid," Christine snapped at the cop. "She said my fucking daughter looks just like my daughter's father! She told my daughter that she knows her father."

The cop didn't expect Christine to be the toniest person, nor did he expect this to be a cake walk so he shook that off and said,

"What else do you remember? Any features?Anything that stuck out?"

"She was light skin, somewhat cute, and my daughter thought she was her friend."

"It's a start but it could be anybody," Moore stated professionally.

Moore's partner asked, "Was there any messages? A ransom note? Did your daughter's father have any enemies?"

"My baby father is a fucking gang leader! Of course he has enemies."

Moore bit his tongue again. "The girl at your house, lets focus on her."

"She was light skin, looks like that chick that used to play on that show, Sun Of The Beach.

$ $ $

A hostess, innocent looking, with endless cocoa legs, nice hips and modest breasts came from behind her podium and said, "And you are?"

"Pierce. I'm here with the Walton party--"

"Oh, Shandy... Right this way," she shot back grinning like a beauty pageant contestant. She had a sumptuous behind and a cute face and moved with an ultra femme flow. Stink followed, eyes wandering, hands in his pockets. The hostess was not only sexy but delicate and dainty with her cascading jet mane. "Here we are," she gushed, stopping before a table of three. Some of Stink's favorite folks.

Stink thanked the hostess, then said, "Your name is?"

"Mona," the hostess replied smiling before turning, taking two steps and nearly twisting her ankle before falling to the floor and writhing in embarrassment. Stink rushed over to her aid, the sparkle of his diamonds removing the staring eyes of many patrons from her. He helped her back to the front of the steakhouse, where she said, "Having dinner with a table full of beautiful women is a regular day for you, I bet."

He replied, "A slow one."

Stink was probably one of the few men unphased by his power, and too busy planning his next move to be resting on his laurels. The hostess noticed his wedding band, not the watch, and instantly stopped the flirting.

"I'll be fine, why don't you join your table."

Upon his return, Azure rose from her chair ready to plant a wet kiss on Stink's lips, but he gave her his cheek. Shandy said, "I think you did a great job at the radio stations, Marcel," her eyes slashing at Azure.

"Even at the end," Azure offered, beaming with joy, "when that girl called in sounding all uneducated."

"Thank you," Stink returned, sitting in a seat between his PR and PYT. "Iris, what's popping with you??"

"You know, just here to show my support," Iris returned, fuming. She did not take too kindly to the developments involving Dave's departure. The case was making waves on Headline News, CNN, and every local station in the Tri-state.

And she was one of the last people he was seen alive with, which meant Dave's driver had to go now. Her leg bounced feverishly bringing the attention of Shandy to the agitated diva.

"Thanks for the support, Iris." He requested a glass of water, guzzled that down, went on to say, "Well, I want to make a couple of announcements that could affect everyone here."

Shandy and Azure were thinking DYNASTY. Each in their

own rite, having been with the don intimately, had aspirations of a happy ending with him. Neither knew about the other's involvement with him, and both thought they were there as his date, even though Shandy had planned the celebratory dinner. The lechery in both their eyes didn't go unnoticed by Iris, all too familiar reality of being in a venue or setting with another girl her man was fucking present. Though she pretended to be approving, it hurt. He wasn't as grandstanding as Stink, but it still hurt. Especially when it came to Christine. The whole scene just nauseated Iris. Two very attractive and educated women salivating at the mouth over a married man. Stink had it going on, that Iris couldn't deny. His waves were spinning, line was sharp, his ice was flawless, and clothes always looked good on him. He looked like money, fresh mint too. And they were his unabashed adorers.

"Ay-yo, what up man?" Iris snapped trying to rush things along. Whatever he was about to say couldn't be more important than what she had to say.

Stink's lip twitched in one of those annoyed ways, then he said, "No matter how often we equate achievement with fortune, money will not forever be a motivating factor. Something else will."

"Yo, you reading from a piece of paper?" asked Iris, shaking her head.

He was. I didn't have a formal education, grew up with no real interest in school. There was a time nothing I knew exceeded the streets, because the underworld has its own language and that's all I needed to know to get anywhere I wanted to go." He drank a little more water, loosened a button at the top of his shirt. "My story of poverty ended many years ago, yet I developed a hunger in other areas of my life. I seemed to struggle more in the last few years than I ever did growing up. I had a vested interest in maintaining the status quo, staying ahead of the pack. Not anymore. It's about societal ambitions, and a moral centerforce."

Iris's foot was bouncing faster, Shandy was moved, jaw agape, and Azure sat eagerly awaiting more.

As Stink prepared to drop the bomb, they were waited on. Shandy peeped something out of the corner of her eye. Not iced Azure's pretty little pump brush up against Stink's leg seductively.

The confident PR with the features of an exotic cat simply smiled. The law student could flirt all she wanted, Shandy mused, certain the night would only end one way. With her ass high in the air, and Stink behind her singing her praises.

Stink read some more of his speech to the women while Azure continued to caress his leg with her foot. Just as he gestured for Azure to cut it out, Iris noticed it. She was about to tell Stink to get to the point, possibly anger him, but her phone chirped. Iris excused herself as Stink said, "Marriage is something that is sacred. I want to work things out with wifie. Also, in order for that to happen, I have to move away. I've decided to run things from the west coast, at least until m y head is right."

Azure didn't believe him, thought she rode his dick too good for him to be serious. Shandy, on the other hand, was paralyzed with shock.

Iris stepped away, and on the other end of her phone Aaliyah could be heard belting out "Can I Come Over." Just an octave above Aaliyah's came a voice Iris hadn't heard in a couple months. Some of the best pussy she'd ever had. Half Black, half

Asian, five-foot-nine with D-cups, and hair that looked wet even when it wasn't. Plans had been in effect to do a threesome, the two of them and Capri once he was released, but the bitch had gone behind Iris's back and wrote him on some groupie shit. A vicious beatdown wouldn't even fix that.

"Bitch, didn't I tell you to lose my number?!" Iris seethed, looking back over her shoulder and every which way, to somewhat shield the foulness seeping from her mouth. "Fuck do you want, you fucking bird?"

A distressed voice replied, "Capri's daughter is missing! It's been all over the news!"

"You little bitch, I will cut your fucking ponytail off with my switch blade! Find something else to play about, and someone else to play with...CLICK I"

The girl called right back, lamented, "I'm serious it's all over the news, bitch!

"You still live in castle Hill, bitch? I'ma come through there and open your fucking head up like I did last time! Keep fucking with me if you wanna!"

"I am not playing. You think I want to feel your wrath again? I am not playing, Iris."

Iris took a deep breath, released it just as the girl said, "They're about to release a composite sketch of the kidnapper." CNN right now! I am not playing!"

Iris sashayed to the bar, her sexy little dress and shoes garnering unwanted attention. Men so far from her type gawked as she climbed her luscious five-three frame up onto the bar stool. Just a few feet from a huge flat screen anchored to the wall, she ordered a drink and purred, "Could you please turn to the news, thanks."

Iris sipped her Corona, and watched just how fast and efficient law enforcement could be when they wanted to be.

The Scarface Dave story "Hijacked Organs" had gone second to the Olivia Hayward developments with the quickness.

Anecdotes from Capri's criminal history were pulled from the archives and plastered tor criticism. He was called a murderer, demented, depraved, a drug kingpin, a psychopath, devil sent. "How did he get five years?" Nancy Grace begged to know. "I'd like to know who tried his case."

Iris watched confused, disoriented. It was like reliving 1997 when he was on the news all the time. This was the last thing Iris needed. And just when she thought things could get no worse, a drawing of the alleged kidnapper was released, along with, "If anybody knows this woman, please contact us toll free at 1-800-Crime-Stoppers."

The camera man swung to the uncountable residents lingering for audience effect, giving the entire country a grand look at Harlem World and one of her many sicknesses. And then whoever was at the news station gave America's viewers another glance at the sketch.

"Yo, that look like you," Stink said, sidling up alongside Iris. Within seconds Stink stared blankly. He was staring up at his comrade's image. Capri Hayward. But that wasn't it. They went from ridiculing him, back to the streets he reigned terror on. Live footage of 143rd Street, a reputable reporter sticking his mic in Christine's face." The mixture of her tears and mascara are clear evidence of the pain this mother is going through," the reporter explained.

Iris said, "Where'd the girls go?"

"They left, went their respective ways."

"Stink, Capri's daughter is missing, and they're talking kidnap. That's what you just walked up on."

"It's gonna fall on us, somehow, some way. Just when I thought I was out, they pull me back in. How long did they say its been?"

"Ten hours ..."

"How much did they ask for?"

"Didn't say. I'm, I'm dumb founded right now. Word up."

Stink stammered, "Who would do this?"

An even better image of the suspect quickly became available. Technology was a mutha!

Iris watched intently, watched as her dude's baby momma played the blame game. Bird ass bitch, thought Iris, irate. Part of her wanted to go through there and slap the shit out of Christine for being so reckless, so undisciplined. She wanted to find Little Olivia and make all this go away. She wondered if Capri had been informed yet, and how he was taking it. She didn't have any babies yet, so she didn't know how it felt to be disconnected from your child. But she knew how it felt to love a man without conditions. So she knew she would inherit his pain whether she wanted to or not.

Stink started making calls and Iris could pretty much hear everything he was saying. The shot caller in him had reemerged with a vengeance, and he had niggas on every corner shaking down their respective neighborhoods. Iris called Zest, and without hesitation he postponed everything he had going on in Atlanta and boarded a redeye to Gothom City.

"There's no contact from the kidnapper, or kidnappers," rifled from the tube. "We'll have full coverage around the clock... back to you, Nancy."

145

like a mausoleum than a gentleman's club.

When Iris returned her hair wasn't flowing anymore. She'd put a pair of Oysters clippers to the sides of her head, and reemerged with a mohawk, the feminine style all the sexy starlets were wearing these days. Any doubts about whether or not she could trust Stink were no more.

Both their phones were blowing up, calls from all over the city.

Iris's mother begged, "Turn yourself in if you wasn't involved, mami. Please" because she didn't have an alibi, or any viable story that could even counter her accusers. "Hell fuckin no, mom!" she lashed out as she took her shoe off.

Stink's street soldiers were unable to give him anything. One of his generals said, "This ain't like the Darnell Porter story. Back then, the streets were talking, them cats thrived off people knowing their work. There ain't a nigga out here crazy enough to take credit for this, Blood."

12 hours! That's how long they were reporting the child missing.

By the time that report was released, Zest was in town. The redeye from Atlanta hit the tarmac at Kennedy around three that morning. He was at the Ruby Red by four, and just kept saying, "Bad timing, bad fucking timing." He had brought along the Georgia boys, with no lark in mind.

It had been some time since these three players took up space in the same room. About a year. And for the first time it wasn't to conspire about taking a life or something that didn't belong to them. It was about bringing the child of their unchallenged leader home, before his wrath came down on them. Capri was much more vicious, far more powerful, and even more calculated than they could ever imagine. And about his beloved daughter, heads were going to roll.

"Stink, did you make contact with Christine?" asked Zest, unconcerned with Iris's feelings at the moment.

"Nah, she all on the news bugging acting wild reckless," Stink bristled. "You hear from her?"

Iris removed herself from the conversation, too painful. She removed her shoes, just paced the hard wood floor, thinking she may never bounce back from this. The last eight years passed before her eyes. The contract killings, the cocaine habit, the love and loyalty she gave Capri.

"For this?" she silently cried. A dream deferred.

By the next morning, 15 hours without any contact from the kidnapper, a story had broke. It was about 5 a.m., the summer sun rising, and they were still hold up in the Ruby Red.

"A moratorium will be placed on Capri Hayward's parole," it said. "He was scheduled to be released in two days," they revealed. "Reputed gang leader and convicted murderer Capri Hayward, will remain in prison, while the authorities work to bring his little girl Olivia Hayward back home. Again, he was scheduled to be released tomorrow, but now it is indefinite. In the interest of the investigation, he will remain in prison."

No one was infallible, no one was flawless, but if ever a time a person's best was needed, it was during tough times. As much as Iris wanted to walk away, maybe charge into the arms of her football player admirer, there was no way she could turn her back on Capri now.

If the D-back saw the news, he probably won't take my call anyway, thought Iris. And even if he doesn't believe I'm responsible, or capable of hurting a child, the idea of me being part of a gang the media were now dubbing the Street Generals, he would easily be over me!

She pursed her lips as the tears began to slowly tumble, thinking she could have been a football wife instead of a true thug's mistress.

"I can't stop, and I won't stop!" she remembered saying in defense of her

choices when probabilities such as these were constantly purported by her mother.

For the first time she wished she'd listened.

CHAPTER SEVENTEEN

The front door collapsed in two powerful strikes from the battering ram. They moved in quickly. About 20 cops, and one FBI agent. Inside was dark, pitch black, until Moore flashed his light.

"In, in, in hurry!" he ordered.

Within minutes they had covered the entire place, and were done scouring the premises.

"There's no one here" a plain clothes cop announced all fired up.

"Any sign of a child being here?" Bob Moore quizzed, fingering a small stack of mail on the stand not far from the front door. Majority of it was bills-- car note, car insurance, cable, cell phone, credit cards. Lots of credit cards, which let Moore know he was looking for a woman that was very high maintenance. From there he visited a mantelpiece heavily decorated with photos. The place was clean, no dust build ups, no dirty dishes, pristine windows, and that let him know that she hadn't been away for long. He wanted to see her bedroom. That's where he was headed when he heard, "We found something!"

"Where?!" Bob Moore returned. One of his close colleagues was coming his way. "W hat is it?"

Moore took a gander, then checked his notes. The first thing that stuck out was pink barrettes. "The little girl was wearing pink barrettes when she went missing.   Where'd you find this?"

"Bathroom, by the bathtub. There's more."

The FBI agent, a middle aged white fellow originally from the New England region, specializing in abduction, said, "I'm right behind you, Detective Moore!"

When Moore got to the bathroom he immediately decided, "Don't touch anything else! Get forensics over here NOW I want Ashford Banks!"

$ $ $

"Sin ain't lie, it was Jason and his faculty, rapping with his back to me Notorious B.I.G. spat, and Five bobbed his head scheming from his tinted hooptie. There was no doubt in his mind somebody had to die. The minute he got the tip that the gates on the Ruby Red were open, he set out to even the score.

The swelling in his head had subsided, the lacerations were healing, but the noise was still there, so he could hear the sound of B.I.G.'s revenge song, but he could also hear the sounds of that explosion.

Slumped down in the front seat, he glared out the wide window of the Mazda minivan. A cutie he recognized from the street life as Everlasting stuck her pretty face out the ajar door as he watched intently. He thought the new mohawk was hot and just added more spunk to the vivacious and outspoken gangstress. Then her whole collection of curves could be seen. "She is a beauty," he was thinking aloud, "even after a long night of doing whatever she was doing in there while I waited out here." Getting fucked!, he imagined.

Next, two brolic dudes with a little bit of height on them he'd had no recognition of showed face, one by one. Stink soon followed, and Five felt the corners of his mouth rise. But the true thrill came when he peeped Zest, as Stink held the fucking door for him to exit like Zest was the don. Five was like a homicidal maniac about to graduate to the big leagues as a ice cold feeling made his body shiver and jolt a little. These guys with their romanticized back-stories, were about to become front page news.

They had no idea they were about to be ambushed, and were actual ly about to act on a tip of their own. Rosa Marie had overheard a conversation at Case Marie that included a name they hadn't heard in a long time. A.J., short for Action Junior.

Stink pulled the gates back down, locked shop up, and as he was activating the alarm system, he heard something big go off. When he turned around he saw a chopper, all black, banana clip, aimed directly at them. The shooter was only 15, maybe 20 yards away, barely visible in the rising sun behind him. The light was blinding, made it nearly impossible to see Five running down on them.

More shots followed!

And Zest was the first to drop.

Iris saw him clutching his throat and blood spilling through his fingers, a look in his eyes she'd never seen before. He was shock. The two visitors from Atlanta rushed to his aid, dragged him behind the rusting bumper of a 1970's four door Oldsmobile. The two massive men were moving quick, and rather easily. Nothing seemed more important to them at that point. The security gate was tattered with bullet holes, and more were coming at rapid speed. There was a thigh strap beneath Iris's skirt, attached to her right leg, and she reached for it. As she clutched, she could not believe that Five didn't have her on his radar.

Five, all 5'5" and 140 pounds of him, was sent flying backwards from the impact of Iris's blazing gun. But he didn't fold, and immediately Iris knew he was wearing body armor.

She sent more shells, this time at his head, and so did he, this time at her mohawk. Iris ducked, and more damage was done to Stink's storefront gates. She looked for Zest, who was halfway down the block now, his black and gray Prada kicks sticking out the back door of a silver Chrysler. Stink was headed in that direction also, his limp limiting his mobility.

More gunsmoke! And that chopping sound was one of a kind. Windows were pierced, shards sent flying. The few bystanders moving about that morning did the best they could to get low.

Iris peeked over the trunk of the car she found refuge behind, and peeped Five moving in just as the shooting ceased.

She saw Five flipping his clip with a devilish smirk on his face.

"Everlasting! Come on!" That was Stink. "Come on!"

Iris couldn't believe Stink wasn't holding heat. The whole legit thing had gone to his head, if he was willing to be caught without it than with it. Iris was caught between watching Stink board the Chrysler Zest had been tossed in, and giving Five everything he wasn't looking for. That split second would cost. "Ev, come on! Lets go! We don't need the heat!" Stink begged, urging her to flee.

Five turned his focus to the Chrysler, the reason he was really there"

About twenty shots entered the driver's side of the Chrysler, leaving them no choice but to pull off without Iris or be swiss cheese.

Five began charging in the direction of the Chrysler, which was running through a red light, shouting obscenities. He fired more shots in that direction, the chopping sound so loud. The Chrysler was hit by an oncoming vehicle, then another before flipping and flipping, and rolling three-and-a-half times before finally coming to rest in the middle of the intersection that connected E. Tremont Ave and Crotona Park East. Bodies flew from the Chrysler. Iris didn't know who, she just went bananas, banging at Five until he hit the ground hard. Her twenty shot piece only had two shots left in the cartridge when she released the trigger.

Blaring horns had replaced the sounds of gunfire. Iris was seething, because she had warned them.

The citizens of East Tremont trudged to their windows, leaving their slumber, their crack pipes, their lovers, to see the carnage the violence had left behind. But not fast enough to see Iris dip into a small alley that lead to the rear of the Ruby Red. She kicked a small bathroom window in, slipped through it, rummaged through a few of the girls' lockers. She tossed a raven wig, Chinese cut, over her mohawk, squeezed into a salacious but cute outfit that belonged to one of the escorts w ho wore her size, then strapped her gat back to her thigh, and proceeded right back through the window she came in just as the cops were coming through the front door. Heavily disguised, no one could finger her as a participant so she went right back to the scene.

Cops were crawling everywhere, ambulance and EMT workers almost matched them in n umbers. No sign of her comrades though. All the spectators standing around giving the crime scene a narrative account from their perspective almost made her miss Five on a gurney, hooked up to a nasogastric tube and IV. They were wheeling him to the back of an ambulance, loading him, read y to shuttle him to the nearest hospital.

Not on Iris's watch!

As they maneuvered the South Bronx streets, she followed closely, thinking hard. Which hospital are they headed to, she wondered. The closest was Lincoln. No, Bronx Lebanon. But they weren't going that way. She continued to tail, finally deciding to pull up alongside the EMT van. The first chance she got, she shouted, "That's my boyfriend in the back! Where y'all taking him?! The closet hospital's Bronx Lebanon!" Something she did not expect happened next. The driver pulled over, and the back door opened up. Iris slammed into park, jumped out of her two-seater, climbed onto the ambulance, and two more shots went off. The EMT workers were not only stunned, but when investigators showed up they had no answers for them. All they could say was, "Sh, sh, she, came onto the ambulance and shot him twice in the face then jumped back off and disappeared..."

$ $ $

Ashford Banks said, "Something seems odd, Bob. This hair, the barrettes, the shoe -- it seems planted."

"That's what I thought," Bob Moore agreed, "that the evidence just seemed too convenient, too available."

The bathroom was connected to the master bed, so Moore wound up in the closet, taking a visual inventory of all the shoes, the furs, designer threads, the jewels, even took a peek in the plentiful panty drawer.

"Didn't know they made gator boots for girls," he muttered, wondering why this vixen would jeopardize everything and for what.

Ashford said, "The child was never here, Bob."

"Someone's setting her up, is what you're trying to tell me, Banks?"

"It is highly possible," Ashford Banks replied. "I'm not even sure we're even hunting the right woman?"

Bob Moore agreed, adding, "This woman is beautiful, very sexy, and obviously not having money problems. Just look around here. Money wouldn't be a motive. She's not a social introvert, she isn't lacking expression, could probably have any man she wants, that is not the characteristics of a kidnapper."

Ashford agreed, a connoisseur of women just like Bob Moore. He went on to say, "Someone brought the evidence here for this very purpose. Someone smart, too. Someone who knows that if this child is never found, this could be enough to lodge kidnap-murder charges, and get a conviction. "

That's why Bob Moore had requested Banks; he was very sharp by many standards, and took pride in his police work. Moore asked, "Anything else stick out to you about this?"

"Besides the fact that no one had made contact with the mot her, requesting a ransom?"

"Besides that..." Bob Moore forced out, his eyes taking in everything the spacious loft had to offer.

"The photos, that's the child's father towering over Iris. I remember seeing him in the news every other day in 1996. Iris Mena is sitting in his lap, with the biggest smile a woman can garner on her face. And that isn't the smile of a fanatic, she's confident. They have a connection, and I think if we find out what that connection is, we find answers to this twist we did not need in this missing child case."

Bob Moore said, "The statistics: eight-hundred-thousand kids go missing every year, a hundred are never recovered, and half of the hundred are found dead."

"Statistics like this make powerful people take matters into their own hands."

"He was supposed to be paroled tomorrow--" began Moore.

"But, someone doesn't want a repeat of what happened the summer of 1996 to happen this summer," Ashford concluded, nodding his head at a slow rhythmatic pace that always aided in his thought process.

"--but, he's liable to com plicate things if he is released."

"Ain't no mystery."

"Was this the work of the guys out in Quantico, NYPD, or the parole board?"

"The parole board could give two shits; recidivism keeps the prison system booming. Like I told you a couple months back, something big's going on."

The FBI agent was taking his own notes, primarily focusing on the photos. It was his theory that the woman they were after wasn't behind the kidnapping. He could be wrong, he secretly noted, but would advance on that theory. One thing he was sure of, it was revenge and not for financial gain, and that's what he'd decided to share with Bob Moore.

"We turned this beautiful woman's beautiful wooden door into splinters, because--?" Bob Moore began.

Ashford said, "The child's mother knows that this woman is involved with Capri Hayward. And there is nothing concrete that says that t his was the woman who she actually saw outside her home?"

"Correct," Moore bristled. "There was no conviction missing from that mother's tone when making her statement. What we are missing here is -- she saw that woman in New Jersey, "he paused for impact. "Little Olivia went missing in Harlem, in the neighborhood Capri and his gang allegedly terrorized."

"If you ever get tired of working in the city, we could use a mind like your's in the bureau," the agent offered. "I've been listening to you and your medical examiner friend toss theories around. And they're plausible. Very."

"Thanks, I'll keep that in mind."

"Where is Iris Mena?" the agent asked, accepting Bob Moore's humbleness. "Her face is all over the news, she has to have seen it or heard of it by now. Think she'll come forward to clear her name?"

"Not if she know's what's been found here at her lovely loft," Moore answered.

"What does she do? Where does she work? Do we know any of that yet?"

Bob Moore said, "Interior design, that's what came up. She has a website and all."

"Pays well," the agent clamored.

"She comes from money, we also know. And it helps that she is the girlfriend of a new millennium definition of a God father."

"Think she knows this? Or is she one of the mail-order girls those guys meet on those penpal websites?"

Those guys were guys Moore had grown up with, guys who made mistakes, even committed some serious crimes, but those guys didn't all deserve banishment, and the Fed sounded like he apparently thought so. That made the statement sound a bit racist,

Moore thought. Moore kept his feelings to himself, and said, "Records show she's been visiting him since December 1996, a month after his arrest, so she isn't a mail-order girl these guys get off a penpal website."

Ashford Banks tagged what little evidence he could gather for Bob Moore, smiling hard inside. The longtime friends were very aware of their Blackness, and conscious of their roots, though neither had a problem screwing a sexy ass white woman every chance they got. As he was removing his black latex gloves, Ashford found out his services were required at yet another crime scene.

"....a woman, in stripper attire, climbed onto the ambulance and shot the victim to death who you   were already attending to for gunshot wounds?"

The EMT worker said, "Yes, there was this scary, evil look in her eyes, that shook me to the core, and then she fired twice. I blinked at the sound of the shots, and in that split second, she was gone..."

Ashford Banks thought this was the most bazaar shit he'd ever heard. It was clear what happened there, cause of death, two shots between the eyes. The scene back on Tremont is what baffled Ashford Banks. A car had been smashed by an oncoming one at approximately 50 mph after being ventilated by dozens of AK-47 projectiles; the car careened and flipped, bodies were tossed from it, but there were no bodies on the scene, and no record of the occupants of the car at any of the hospitals in the surrounding area. Ashford was left scratching his chin, and waiting for a call back from his good chum.

Bob Moore had been asked to accompany the FBI on a trip up to Attica to visit a tough guy of mammoth proportion. If they were to save his daughter, he would be the key.

But Capri Hayward had decided he didn't want to see anyone without talking to his attorney first. He didn't care that it involved his only child. He was pissed. Not only was his parole snatched, but so was his phone privileges, and he'd been removed from general population. What he didn't know was they were also planning to move him to downtown Manhattan County Courthouse, and right across Centre Street, was the federal courthouse. It was one of those places criminals dreaded.

Moving Capri was like moving Jason Voorheese. The 220 pounds on his six foot frame looked more like 275. The pullup bar, those pushups and dips, incorporated with his powerlifting and cardio routines, Capri was massive. Couple that with the fact that he was supposed to be a free man, a man who believed that he'd beat the system. He wasn't trying to cuff up, he was seething obscenities like a pirate on the Black Sea. And there was no relenting until he had confirmation from the warden's secretary that his lawyer would meet him there.

She was a sloppily built woman who always wore cheap clothes, shoes and perfume, an over-made-up face and hairdos but, did her job very effectively. So when she came to Capri's holding cell in the solitary wing and said, "I spoke to Mr. Savino personally, Mr. Hayward." He believed her.

"And I hope that your little girl's returned to your family safely, Mr. Hayward," she added, holding back a thick file in one hand, while using the other to touch a tress on her blonde wig.

"Yeah, whatever, fuck out of here, slut!" Capri snapped back, believing the whole world had just turned against hi m. Everyone except his lawyer. It was also his way of let ting the authorities know they could and would never break him. He was rich in spirit, and a scholar at survival.

This lawyer genuinely liked Capri Hayward. No one knew exactly why though. The kid had money, and brought plenty of it to "Rodolfo, Manning and Savino," but that wasn't it. All three defense attorneys thought their famed firm would suffer a hit when Action turned up dead, but actually took a hike in business and revenue after taking on Capri Hayward as a client.

Again, it wasn't the money. Immediately upon meeting him, Savino knew Capri wasn't the average hustler from upper Manhattan like most of the characters shuffling into their Park Place offices. Capri was a gangster through and through, high in energy and could hold a conversation with anybody about anything. Capri had even made Savino fantasize about living on the wrong side of the law, that's how fascinating Capri was to him. And Savino had worked with some formidable figures, real heavy hitters in his time.

On top of that, in his heart, Savino knew Capri was guilty of some of those homicides he got him off for. "It is just so much easier working for guys who don't run their mouths," Savino had once said in regards to his professional responsibility or lack thereof.

Savino arrived at the Tombs expecting nothing other than Capri's militant aura. But when he saw Capri he immediately noticed heavy bags beneath his eyes, and circles as dark as a raccoon's. "Pri, what's up man?" he asked before the guard had even afforded them their attorney-client privacy.

"My little girl is missing, gone, 36 hours now," Capri thugged out, "and I ain't slept in two days, Joe."

"They brought you here because they believe you have too much power." Savino cleared his throat. "And, because someone

164

from the FBI, and someone from Major Crimes would like to talk to you."

"About what??? I ain't got no rap."

"Finding your daughter!"

"And that's it?"

"I wish!" Savino sulked, taking a seat. He removed his wire frames, said, "You will remain in solitary confinement until they find your little girl, dead or alive."

Capri sighed, saying, "I know the statistics; eight-hundred-thousand go missing every year, one hundred are never found, and half that hundred come up dead."

Savino loosened the pinstriped tie around his thick white neck, released the two buttons on his dark sports jacket and said, "So, you, you wanna talk to them? I'll sit in the entire time, man."

Reluctantly, Capri nodded, his eyes bloodshot red.

CHAPTER EIGHTEEN

Iris was in a state of shock, this otherworldly feeling surrounding her. She had never done anything so daring, so dangerous, so dumb. There was no doubt in her mind, she could be identified. But seeing Zest leaking from his pharynx was like seeing a rusty water pipe burst in her face. In her eyes, she had no choice but to act accordingly. Now she was in a car with the E on her dash for the gas blinking, scared to death to stop and fill up, fearing someone would recognize her and call the cops. She couldn't go to her parents' home because the cops had been there twice already and had a cruiser parked right, out front. A neighbor text her and wrote, "The police have invaded your loft." No calls from her boys. Rosa hadn't heard from Stink, and was bugging about what she was witnessing all over the news. Yeah, the Ruby Red had been raided and the cameraman was sending feeds straight to NEW YORK 1 News with a veteran correspondent trying to paint a picture of what happened earlier that morning.

There was only one person Iris could call.

The half Black, half Asian chick answered her phone on the first ring. Iris said, "Hey."

"Where are you, bitch?"

"Mimi, I didn't do it."

"I know how much you love that niggah. Where you at?"

"About five minutes from you."

"Park your car in the back, and I'll meet you by the back exit.

"I got you."

"I'm on my way."

"I know, and I can't wait to see you. Hurry up."

Iris thought Mimi sounded too eager to please her, too fast to be about her when they weren't even on the best of terms. Mimi knew the price of everything, but the value of nothing.

Iris had her reservations about the move, but found herself reluctantly traveling towards the Castle Hill projects. Mimi knew how to eat pussy, and never left the butthole out when crawling between Iris's legs. Paid very close attention to breasts and lips, and was incredibly great at giving orgasms.

That could take Iris's mind off things for a minute -- a little bit of carnal futzing with a sure sensualist in the midst of adversity -- right? But the reality was outside of sexuality. Iris had nothing in common with the print model with the penchant for clubbing and shopping.

Iris was still in disguise, and that got her unwanted attention the minute she stepped foot out of the car in them platform shoes and little ass booty shorts. Young, juvenile dudes with aging hormones started whistling at her, shooting their best game. Because of who she was down with cat calls were foreign to Iris.

She kept her composure, but damn near jumped out her skin when her phone chirped. A smile crossed her lips when she recognized the number.

"Iris, where are you?"

"Shamari--?"

"I wanna help you. I have OTA's right now, but you can go

out to my place and I'll meet you there as soon as I'm done here. Okay?"

"I don't want to complicate things for you, when you're getting ready for training camp, Shamari. "

"The key is under the mat out back. Go there, please. I know you didn't do this. Look, I have to go, coach is calling. I don't believe you did that, Iris."

Mimi had come to the back door of her project building anyway, and she and Iris were looking directly at each other, eyes locked, separated by about thirty feet. Iris began to back pedal, looking sexy even when she was uncomfortable. 'I'm going there now, Shamari."

He whispered, "I'm going to cook you something nice," before hanging up.

"Iris! Where are you going?" Mimi bellowed, exiting the rear of her building in short shorts, a pink tank-T with no bra, and some Gucci flipflops.

"Come here!"

"Don't worry! I'm good!" Iris shouted back. As she deactivated the alarm, grabbed the door handle, eased back behind the steering wheel, she noticed five burly figures, plain clothes, running across the large parking lot. "Cops!" she shrilled, slamming the door behind her, and scrambling to put the key in the ignition. They were moving fast, faster than she was. Cars began to converge, tires screeching, feet pounding the concrete.

She was boxed in. And the look in her beautiful eyes was like that of an exotic animal about to be taken from its native land for the purpose of making fur coats for the rich and famous.

Obscenities began to flow from Iris's mouth, and they were directed at Mimi.

A soft spoken fellow, short on breath, said, "Step out the car. Please. The easier the better."

Iris shook her head, fighting hard to prevent the tears from escaping her soul. The E on the dash was the only reason she surrendered. More obscenities came, directed at Mimi.

The soft spoken fellow, catching up with his breath, - said, "It wasn't shorty, lil mama." Then a van pulled up, and they shuffled Iris to the open door.

$ $ $

Bob Moore looked like a street thug to Capri. The agent, though husky with broad shoulders, looked weak and manipulative. And in comparison to Joe Savino, his suit looked terribly cheap. Capri saw the agent as one of those dudes who thought being blessed was being just a little smarter than his friends or colleagues.

On the way back down to the city, all agreed that Bob Moore would initiate all dialogue. The first thing he said was, "Do you have any enemies that you'd like to tell us about?   Something we can go on right now?"

"I have no enemies."

"What about money? Did you owe any money?"

"I don't owe niggas... shit."

"Ah, Iris Mena, we're ready to rule her out as the kidnapper. What do you think about that?"

"I never thought she did it. I was actually with her the week before last, about a couple weeks ago. "

"She visited you?" "Looking real good too."

"Were you surprised when you heard she was the person of interest? The person possibly holding your daughter captive?"

169

and left the country for our neighbors."

"That's right, Canada!" Moore blasted. "What are the chances of her being in the country, being the woman Christine saw outside her home?"

The agent said, "Did your interview yield anything about the triple murder involving a federal agent?"

"No," the prosecutor replied.

"Hey, what about this kid? Is she not a priority anymore? I thought that's why we were here? Has the agenda changed and I'm the last one to know?!" Moore was pissed. It seemed like things again had all of a sudden become about race. "A fucking child is out there missing, and that is a priority to me!"

"It is to us too, it's just unfortunate that the kidnapping just opened back up an old wound."

"You know what that sounds like to me?"

"What?"

Moore said, "Social neglect!"

Her response was simple and plain, vanilla in her world, "Come on, Moore. This is not about race, this is about opportunity." With a cute round face, a button nose, almond shaped eyes, and about forty years on her lifespan, the lithe prosecutor awaited Moore's response.

He growled, "I guess racial complexities still do exist, and in some ways we are still slaves, the only change being the terms of our servitude! And guess what? I don't work for the Bronx District Attorney's office."

"Moore," she called, "this is a joint borough effort.

Manhattan and the Bronx! So you do work for me!" "Well, I'm going to find that little girl!"

"Just listen. We've pieced together a picture of the Generals, its size and structure, allies and enemies, the way they move, and exactly how to corner them."

Moore turned around, his brown hand in the grasp of the prosecutor's white one. As she relinquished him, he said, "How did you guys come up with the name for this crew?"

"They make their own rules, they are all leaders in their own rite, and they commanded the respect and fear of the streets one way or the other, by committing crimes that dwarf that of Action and his crew. Street soldiers don't have the tenacity or the charisma."

"I thought they were gang bangers."

"They are, but to categorize them as just such would downplay the sophistication they possess."

The agent said, "Don't take this the wrong way, but they've found what we've hidden in the books."

The D.A. picked up, "Gangbangers are thoughtless, careless, and a majority of the time unjustified."

$ $ $

The soft spoken fellow had a Breitling Limited Edition, gold and iced out, on his left wrist. A red gold rosary around his neck with white diamonds all through the crucifix. He also had a wedding band on his left hand with stones in it. She could not believe they had Juelz Santana's album playing, or that one of them was rapping along not missing a lyric.

"Who the fuck are y'all? Damn sure ain't no fucking cops! "Not wanting to immediately allude to the alarming discrepancies she'd noticed, she said, "I'm not even cuffed! Cops would have cuffed me! No Miranda rights? What am I even being detained for? I didn't do anything!"

No one spoke to her, just continued on the bumpy ride vibing to Santana.

Could they be Scarface Dave's people?, she wondered.

Or, had some other foul act she had banked off of finally caught up with her?

Whoever they were, they had convinced an entire parking lot of project heads that they were acting in the interest of their safety.

She continued shooting her shit, trying to solicit info to no avail. Iris was irate now, straight vexed. "I want to speak to my lawyers!"

$ $ $

Joe Savino hated having to do this, but it had to be done. The door shut behind him slowly, and Capri sat upright. He'd been in that chair for two hours now, and hoped Savino could tell him something that favored him, something that was positive about his daughter.

"There are two types of conspiracies in New York state law, Capri. One, a lesser degree, carrying 2 - 6 years. And the other must first prove a basic conspiracy charge when two or more persons agree to commit a crime and perform two or more actions in furtherance of that crime. The act doesn't even have to be criminal."

"What are you telling me?"

"A guy can dust snow from the windshield of a car for his buddies who're using the car to commit a crime. He doesn't even have to get in the car."

"I was told that my parole was being put on hold until I spoke with the investigators. I spoke," Capri barked, his hands in fists.

"Now the more severe conspiracy has a third prong. If the co-conspirators are over eighteen--"

"I don't want to hear this shit!"

"--and involve a minor under sixteen in their illegal activities, then the conspiracy itself is a charge, a top felony, carrying 8 - 25 years. This is a A-1 felony."

"I did my time, bee," Capri deadpanned rising from his uncomfortable seat ing arrangement.

"Do you remember BB, crushed by a moving car? He was fifteen, and he died while with you?"

"Joe, BB was my little man, I paid for his funeral. I gave his mother some money to get out of the ghetto."

"I know what type of guy you are. You don't have to prove that to me. The government's looking to mount a case saying he was more than your little man, that you two were actually acting as co-conspirators when he was run over by that vehicle. I told you this could come back up, that there's no statute of limitation on homicide."

"I'm supposed to be popping champagne and getting my dick sucked tomorrow, Joe!" Capri spazzed. "But that all changed when my daughter went missing! I have to get out there for her now."

"With the mounting sophistication, bringing closure to an era is as promising as life itself, and the government is ready to prosecute you again, Pri."

"You can't be serious? You gotta make this go away! And what about them trying to find my daughter?"

"There's a cop hellbent on bringing little Olivia home. He was out there making sure they understood that that was the priority."

"The cat who said I wasn't going anywhere until they found my daughter?"

"Yes, him. Fiery guy."

"Yo, I'm sick right now! What can you do to make this go away! I gotta get out there. I lost my moms an pops, I ain't trying to lose my daughter."

"I never had a problem shaping or punctuating legal arguments, of course, based on a battery of facts. And I'm a phenon at interpreting law. We just don't have much to stand on as we speak, Capri."

"25 years?"

"If convicted, yes that is the max."

"Conspiracy to my little man's death? That is bugged out."

"That may be just the beginning."

Clearly Capri was agitated. And that's why Savino said what came next. His job was to give his client the best opportunity to be successful, and that's what he was thinking.

"I have to tell you this, Capri," he started, then cleared his throat, "there's a deal called Queen-for-a-day."

"And what the fuck is that?"

"A defendant can spill his guts to prosecutors without self-incriminating himself, off the record without fear..."

"You just lost me!"

"If you know anything, now's the time to tell me. Just tell the truth when it's convenient to do so. And I'll handle the rest."

"As sure as God's earth is green... a day will never come when I break the code."

"I know, I know Capri."

"I got a plan though. And it's a whole lot in it for you."

178

"A whole lot, meaning?"

"A million dollars."

"This isn't one of those--"

"A mill, man!"

"And what do I have to do?"

Capri wrote it down, and slid the piece of paper across the table.

Savino could make a million without Capri, but he'd have to split it three ways... after Uncle Sam takes his half, which would leave Savino with a little less than $167,000. This was the perfect opportunity to supplement his taxpaying salary. Savino said," Two mil, and we got a deal."

CHAPTER NINETEEN

Christine was really just a child trapped in a woman's body. Dating Capri had rushed her maturation, almost like a kid corning straight out of high school to play for a hall of fame coach on a pro team. No college experience, no real life skills. The bar was that high, trying to keep up with a goon of Capri's stature. And then almost overnight she had to prepare to be someone's mommy.

It wasn't in her plans, none of it was, at least not that soon. Especially not becoming a prisoner's wife in her second trimester. She had expected to be lavished with gifts, taken on trips, pampered like the other ghetto celeb girls with no true challenges to face. Little did she know. Prior to meeting Capri, she was into boys, promiscuous with crushes, given gifts, but free of fault, free to be carefree when she chose to be. She knew she could never have those days back, but it didn't stop her from fantasizing about it.

Mecca watched from the far end of the room, watched her eldest daughter serve in and out of a catatonic state, while nursing a Newport 100 and a shot glass of scotch. It was now 48 hours. Exactly two days. Two days of drinking and chain smoking. Two days of no dialogue between her and Christine. Two days of nonstop news coverage. Police and reporters were camped out on   143rd Street. Christine wanted to leave so baa, go home and just curl up in her bed, but she feared that if she left Harlem, that Olivia would be returned and she wouldn't be there and Olivia would hate her forever for abandoning her. Olivia was seven going on seventeen, wise beyond her years. And that just scared Christine even more because she knew that Olivia knew how to piss someone off. She had that unpredictable gene like her father.

Phones were situated throughout the project apartment, two detectives and voice analysis experts were flanking a highly recommended negotiator, though no one expected any negotiations to go down. This was just a huge case, and highly publicized, so the authorities pulled no stops.

The doorbell rang, and Christine gasped. There   stood   a gawky looking fellow in a delivery outfit, and as soon as the door opened he said, "Someone order a pizza with anchovies and Canadian bacon?"

Christine charged at the fellow, and had to be restrained.

"Don't nobody in here eat no fucking Canadian bacon and anchovies!" she cried out hysterically.

One of the detectives took the pizza, opened the box, and as sure as the heavens above was home to the Father, there was a postcard inside. The poor pizza guy was tackled and detained. And as soon as this word traveled, the young boys downstairs, unable to be denied, flipped the delivery truck over.

Back upstairs, the postcard said, "Are you free of fear? Are you being graceful under the pressure? Olivia is. Just like her daddy. But you, Christine, I bet you're afraid to go on?"

As the delivery guy was being interrogated and more than forthcoming, the phone rang. "They want Christine!"

181

jammed inside her.

His pace picked up, as did her's. By the time they made it to the bed, the scent of sex was in the air and Patience had climaxed twice. They took a brief break, and Patience filled a glass twice with Clicguot, then told dude, "I want it from the back. Doggystyle."

The guy from the midtown winery gave it to her just the way she wanted it. His college friends would never believe him if he told this story, so it was this moment that mattered, and he busted his second nut hoping she remembered him like he'd remember her.

Finally, he collapsed on the bed with Patience's DNA all over him, and his stockpile in a condom.

Patience rolled over on her side and they were facing each other. "You okay?"

"I had the time of my life," he revealed.

"What did you like most?" she asked, giggling softly.

He said, "The way you sucked me off. I guess one can really think things into existence."

Patience chortled again. "How much did you like it?"

"So much that a man who has mastered his emotions feels so vulnerable."

Patience shoved him onto his back and mounted him. She felt his hardness against her naked thigh and said, "You want another blow job, don't you?"

He nodded as he corralled her breasts.

"Say it."

"Sounds like you want me to beg."

Patience said," I do. Now beg me, right now."

"Give me another blow job."

"No, be nasty about it, be bossy like a gangster."

"I can't," he bristled." I'm not a gangster or a boss."

"Then get ready, we're done."

"Okay, okay... He took a deep breath. "Suck my dick."

Patience grinned, in control. As she re-wrapped his dick with that strawberry latex, lowered her mouth over his twitching dick head, all across the shaft and balls, she wondered what Capri was doing at that very moment, and how different their lives may've been had he been a little more patient with her, and a lot more loyal to her.   But he'd been everything but exemplary. The guy from the winery stammered, "You're like a pro...fessional. It's like the condom isn't even there. Shit!... Fuck!... Damn!" Then his body spasmed.

Simpering, she replied, "I'll take that as a compliment."

Capri's good girl had gone bad, and he would never know just how much his decisions had affected his no longer simpatico ex. She could spend the rest of her life trying to get back the nine years she gave to the beautiful soul, but a demented mind of Capri Hayward. No one knew exactly how much was raging beneath her surface.

The guy didn't know what was driving him more crazy, the sensational feeling of Patience's luscious lips and thick tongue, or the lecherous look in her hazel eyes.

At that very moment Capri was in his cell staring at four walls composed of cinder block. A cell that felt and appeared as though it hadn't been cleaned in months. The stainless steel finished sink/toilet combination had defied its purpose.

Brillo couldn't help that mess. Capri took a gander at the sheets and pillowcase that was already there when he arrived, and immediately opted to rest on the bare mattress which wasn't much cleaner. And because it was early-August, the ventilation system wasn't just pushing out recycled stale air, but the air was ice cola. If ever a place could be unwelcoming, this was the place.

He began to pace and think of his only child and the hell the people responsible would pay once it became clear who was behind this. The pace was slow and steady, and because he was six feet tall, it didn't take many steps to cover the nine feet from the front of the cell to the back. He wondered how Christine would try to explain this, or would she just leave now that the only thing holding them together was gone, and every news broadcaster, every media personality was verbally flogging him, some even banishing him. Capri chuckled, but he really wanted to breakdown. He'd had to be strong for too, too long; since before puberty.

While others had mothers to smother them with affection, the streets would be the only provider of that provision for Capri. He led a wild life of thuggery while living vicariously through memories, and allowing his easily malleable mind to be molded by the man he'd later learn could've prevented his mother's murder.

His cell was basically away from all the others; it was at the farthest end of the tier where no one could see or hear him, and he could see nor hear anyone. There, after nearly two decades of holding things in, he was ready to burst, let it all out, all the pinned up pain, all the years of frustration, the lack of a maternal bosom, all the carnage he witnessed or administered. Now he had failed his daughter, and could do nothing about it.

He was about to collapse to his knees and let it all out when he heard footsteps and keys on the other side of the door keeping him confined.

Quickly, he took a powerful stance, crossed his arms over his massive chest and waited at the small window in the door for his visitors to appear, walk into his icy glare.

A corrections officer approached a captain and someone in plain clothes flanking either side of him. The C.O., a hood fellow, was carrying a manila envelope. He said, "The deputy warden and the captain would like to speak with you."

The deputy warden was a woman of African decent, and she had a   fake-ass smile on her face.

Capri, in his revolutionary state, spat, "Then open the door!"

"You know I can't do that."

The woman stepped up and said, "Your daughter has been returned home safely. It's all over the news."

The reaction was a delayed one. Though it wasn't something he would openly confess, he didn't expect to ever see his daughter again. Now that she was back in the bosom of her mother, that didn't mean his problems ended, and he knew this, they were only beginning. "Good, now let me the fuck out of here he said through a sigh of relief and blend of cockiness that didn't go unnoticed. "I got some calls to make!"

There was no immediate response, only a shift of standing arrangements amongst the prison officials. "Mr. Hayward, you won't see population here, the captain announced, a black man of mammoth size, now front and center. "Won't be no spring cleaning going on around here. And if it were up to me you'd be confined for the rest of your life, no contact with the outside world. Give him his mail."

The captain and the deputy started back towards the stairs before Capri could jar their sensibility, spit some vulgar

You hide behind the facade, your capabilities, your looks and little mystique, as though that's going to add some real depth to your character. The money, the respect, the power you got in the streets and prison really holds no true weight if you have an imbalance inside.

I thought I was giving enough so that you wouldn't have to go searching for any fucking thing else. But you chose this slut bitch, yeah, the one in the photos my P.I. was able to capture for your eyes Capri. Violating whatever little understanding y'all had. Oh, that's right, you gave her a baby! Thought Homie's babymothers were off limits! Ain't that one of the laws y'all live by. I gotta go. I got me a nice dick to spit and sit on. The photos got me a little wet, Pri.

Pri knew exactly who the mail was from. And the only thing that had ever hurt more than that very moment was when he found out his mother had been murdered. He was barely a teen at the time. He was more mad at himself, for mishandling Patience, the way things ended, and for Christine and Stink fucking around behind his back. He'd always known something was going on, but in some twisted way of seeking redemption for the unjust murder of Lux, he had given Stink a pass. Had he grown, developed a conscious? Hell no! Had they been out in the open, just blatantly shitting on him, his hand would've been forced.

But seeing those photos, he felt compelled to show them he was better than them. He felt like the world was watching. But, with no access to a phone, there was nothing he could do, but suck it up. Unless his lawyer came through on their deal.

CHAPTER TWENTY-ONE

"We're in the dog days of summer, but it's turned out to be a Godly one for a Harlem mother," one reporter rhymed looking into the lense of a camera, with a large crowd playing the backdrop to her live coverage of the reuniting of mother and child.

Little Olivia was back in the bosom of Christine, not a hair on her head harmed and with a full stomach. There wasn't much family around her because she didn't have much, and the people who did want to see her wouldn't dare approach with all the law enforcement around. Bob Moore was at the press conference as well as his higher-ups, such as x, the Police Commissioner, and the Mayor of New York City.

Investigators had their notepads out, but nothing to go on in them.

Christine just wanted them to all go away, take her daughter home and never let her out of her sight again. A thought came to her mind. When Little Olivia was really little, when she was withdrawn, when she wouldn't speak and seemed angry all of the time, and people close to them told Christine that Olivia may've been autistic. She was a late bloomer, expressed herself differently than other kids her age, but there was nothing slow about Little Liv. And as Christine stood there, somewhere she didn't want to be, she watched her daughter take the shine,

It was late afternoon now and East Tremont Avenue had been cleaned of the wreckage. There was still a lot of detectives and technicians around, and the Ruby Red was still a place of interest, though nothing incriminating could be found.

The bullet holes in the security gate was really the only reason they were there. The hunch was, "Whoever ran this joint, or whoever came here for fun, that person or persons, male or female, was the target."

"This isn't a joint," said a ATF agent in his thirties who also happened to be from the struggle. "Somebody brought the Borgata to the Bronx. The roulette table, the poker tables, the bar and stages, as good as any real casino."

"Everything's red," said another agent.

"And the only thing out of order -- the broken window in the bathroom. Not sure if someone broke it trying to get out, or in."

"The owner is Rosa Pierce."

"She also owns that new hot restaurant on the Grand Concourse."

Bob Moore walked up and said, "Is she okay? Anybody check on that?"

"She's fine."

"What about her husband?" Bob Moore boomed. "This is his joint, according to an informant I interviewed this morning."

"Well, we understand she wasn't very cooperative and we have no reason to encourage anymore. She did say that her husband is fine."

"The guy who was killed in that ambulance, by a woman who we believe works here -- I was at his mother's apartment a few weeks ago. The car bombing led me there. But the car isn't in his mother's name. It was in a stripper named Scarlet's name. Scarlet's boyfriend was stripped of his organs, then killed."

"Six degrees of separation," the ATF agent sounded off.

"There's more, we understand he was last seen with a woman fitting the same description. We find this woman, we find our killer, and maybe her employer."

THE FINALE CHAPTER

What fucking luck, thought Iris.

Turned out it wasn't NYD who'd snatched her up in Castle Hill projects; it was an extraction team tailored to intervene on behalf of affluent parents with children spiraling out of control, hoping to rescue their progeny from the perils of the streets before they were completely destroyed. Most times it was a rebellious daughter caught in the throes of a ruthless pimp; other cases involved trust-fund brats looking to be romanced only to be bilked by a fast talking street player with bad habits his pretty prey eventually inherits.

Iris's folks had different worries. They weren't losing sleep because they didn't know if Iris was being beaten to death, infested with drugs, or slowly losing her soul on a ho stroll. They actually thought highly of Iris, though they were aware of her cocaine habit and tax free finances. Intervention became imminent when their only child's face had become a catapult for TV ratings.

A friend with hopes of becoming the Empire State's next governor had recommended the outfit, mostly composed of retired athletes. Abigale Ophilia Orr, the rich governor-hopeful, had enlisted them some time back when her seventeen-year-old daughter nearly ruined her political career on an inadvertent smear campaign. When they found the lush runaway, she was strung out on heroin and peddling pussy nonstop out a flat in the Polo Grounds. Her pimp was one of those vicious new wave bruisers with an affinity for young white gals, so rescuing the natural red-head required skill and patience. The extraction had garnered much delight and dividends for the all black crew.

The Serenity Recovery House was intense and very therapeutic, ran with very little tolerance by a crew of directors, mostly composed of whites -- but Iris fell right in knowing it was necessary.

"REHAB?! " she had initially deadpanned, thinking very little, if any, of the cancerous behavior she'd been subject to or the consequences. She couldn't get Capri out of her mind, and with no outside contact, no cable or network television, and around the clock counseling, she had no id ea what his world was corning to. She had already given up the white lines. But she was beginning to realize that coke wasn't her only disease. Capri was a drug, addictive and hazardous to her health. He and his entire faction were really no good for her.

A couple of druggy brats from Long Island with silver spoons still in their mouths tried to give Iris a hard time when she first pulled up, not knowing Iris wasn't fodder or against fooling. But they quickly realized she wasn't the average when Iris flung an open hand at the leader, a tall busty blonde with blue eyes and butt injections, before retreating to her room the second night there.

She wondered how such a tiny room with a teeny window could have such a stunning Niagra Falls vista. She was just one of fifteen inpatients wishing they were in the comfort of their own abodes. The discomfort made Iris ponder about her loft and who would pay for the damages done to her front door. Something small, she figured, in contrast to the crimes she committed to acquire the quarters and the contents enclosed, or probably disclosed.

Little did she know, her parents had also sent in a repair man to put in a new door while they straightened up. To further encourage uprightness, they were there to corral her after 21 days of treatment.

Iris didn't go right back to the city, though she wanted to badly. But the urge quickly vanished when she learned Stink had changed his number. That was all he had changed. Iris happened to catch him on television talking about his nonprofit and his plans to change the racial disparity within the judicial system. He also mentioned his plans to give away ten full scholarships to college to start the next calendar year, paid for by Accountability Where It Counts. His publicist was there too, in obvious awe of the man after he dissed her only a month ago. For the first time since meeting Stink, Iris saw him as a con artist, a manipulating opportunist, as diabolical as Capri, the one who says, "If there's ever anything you can do for me let me know."

Iris turned channels, then crossed her ankles, right over left. She was lounging in some sweats and a wife beater, no bra or shoes. Her hair was pulled back in a loose and low ponytail, and jewelry was the furthest thing from her mind. She still managed to look noteworthy, and would have no problem upstaging any chick. But one look at her feet and she was out purchasing a French-tip pedicure. A manicure was in order too, hands looking all ratchet. The Asian woman working on her didn't speak much, didn't smile either, but she knew a good makeover when she saw one. In a choppy delivery, she said, "Nice. No corn, no bunion.

You man going to like nice feet, nice hand too."

As Iris was leaving the Astoria, Queens nail salon, in her thong sandals, fedora hat and shades, she passed a newsstand and a familiar face caught her eye.

Famed attorney Joe Savino, caught trying to smuggle a designer suit, prosthetic mask with the likeness of an all-American man, loaded Glock and a cellphone into Tombs on official visit with client Capri Hayward -- the first paragraph read. The second paragraph said, Just a week ago Hayward had been indicted by the FBI in a multiple homicide case that had gone cold for 8 years, as well as conspiracy for gang activity in two boroughs.

The treatment program gave Iris the ability to identify addiction, the traits, and avoid objectifying those vices which would make her weak and vulnerable, and eventually unhealthy again.

Iris dropped the paper back on the newsstand, and moved into a slow but sultry gait that exuded confidence, the beaming sun above making the fresh paint on her toes and fingers glow like rubies.

When she got home, there was an envelope under her door. A big envelope. Didn't say who sent it, or where it had come from. Special delivery, that's it. Iris was skeptical at first, and then the content made her blush, get all warm inside, almost like a schoolgirl having her first crush finally acknowledge her. It was a ticket to a football game. The seat was in the third row, about ten yards from the goal post where she could see the players score and celebrate.

This wasn't exactly romantic, but it was the only thing a man had ever done even remotely close.

Two days later Iris was on her way to New England wearing a football jersey. Cornerback Shamari Jason was making his first start in a AFC East Showdown. Iris had never been to New England, never worn a football jersey, or even been to a sports event for that matter, but it was time to get out the city, time to start doing new things, healthy things, things she wouldn't feel bad about afterwards.

Shamari was a good observer, Iris knew immediately upon meeting him, and it showed during the game because he was reading the quarterback's eyes, constantly jumping the throwing lanes and batting down balls that September afternoon. Eventually, in the third quarter, trailing by 3, he caught an interception he took back 37 yards for a touchdown. Iris jumped out of her seat cheering for him as he blew her a kiss. They would only hold the lead briefly, and eventually lose 20-17. But Shamari was still a winner because that nig ht Iris gave her full attention to a man who wanted it, who'd waited for it, who would appreciate it.

"We could do this every weekend," Shamari voiced.

Iris agreed. But she knew she could never truly transition without seeing Stink first. He knew too much about her, and she didn't know enough about him.

Bright and early that Monday morning, Iris rolled out of Shamari's arms and located her bikini cut panties.

"Where you going?" asked Shamari, watching her slip into the black silk bottoms then her bra. "I don't ever want you to leave."

"Something I hav'ta do," she replied softly and smiling affectionately the entire time she got dressed.

"Right now?"

"Yes, right now. "

"You're going to be happy and free to live and be who you want to be, and I'm gonna see to it."

"Not if I don't go take care of this," Iris replied, fastening the top two buttons of her jeans.

"You are so fucking gorgeous. In and out of clothes." Iris whispered in a breathy tone he liked, "So are you; all of you."

Shamari was wrapped up in a Versace sheet from the waist down, but Iris had no problem locating his penis as she kissed his lips, saying, "I'll be right back, I promise, for more of you mind, soul and dick."

"I'm not moving from here 'til you get back," he replied helping himself to a handful of her fat ass. "So hurry up!"

Shamari's pricy pad was in the Garden State, just one town over from Stink's sprawling mansion.Iris did the speed limit there while listening to the stereo. She was beaming the entire her drive, jolts of ecstasy still flowing through her body. Shamari was kind, attentive, passionate, he paid close attention to every inch of her body. He kissed her toes, her ass. He made her chant his name, tears escape her soul. He made her wish all the good things in the world happen to him, and only him. She could still feel him sliding in and out her warm gash as she pulled up to Stink's place, uninvited.

Two cars took up much of the space on the horseshoe shaped driveway. Rosa's Benz coupe and Stink's sedan. Everything seemed normal, except for the loud music that got louder with each step Iris took towards the front door. Heavy Metal wasn't their style, but that's what was playing. Iris knew ringing the bell would be frivolous, so she just rapped her fist against the large wooden door. When no one answered, she headed around back.

There wasn't another residence in sight, and at least 100 yards separated each home.

She peeked through the sliding glass door when she got around back. Nothing seemed out of place, except the music, which was screaming for attention now.

She was only there to see where she and Stink stood, since things had been hostile the last time they shared space. Zest's condition wasn't even a factor anymore. So, the visit could wait another day or two, her announcement would probably be better prepared too, she figured.

With those thoughts in mind, Iris decided to make her way back to her car, back to Hudson County and the man waiting in bed for her.

Just as she turned on her pivot, a hand reached for the glass door. The hand was about a foot from the ground, reaching up. The hand left a print on the glass, a bloody print.

Iris squatted down in slow motion, and locked eyes with... Rosa. "Oh shit!" she buzzed, seeing if the sliding glass door would open.

It did!

Rosa was naked and barely clinging to life.

Iris said, "What happened, mami?"

"They shot him, a lot," Rosa forced out, gasping hard.

Whoever they were had shot Rosa too, in the head, but miraculously the bullet didn't penetrate her skull, as very little blood trickled down from the hole in her blonde do. She was still in very bad condition, Iris realized, having spotted two more holes in Rosa's back, and the blood flowing from them.

"Where's Stink?" Iris asked.

Rosa's response was faint-- "Living room."

When Iris located Stink, he was nude as well. And yes, they had shot him a lot, shot him to death. His chest was open, as was the side of his head.

Iris's hand went to her mouth and nose to avoid the scent of death permeating the place. The move was also out of sheer shock of the carnage. He'd been dead for a while, which told Iris that Rosa had been holding on for as long as she could.

She took one last look, then moved swiftly back to where Rosa was.

Iris had one foot in and one foot out the rear of the mini mansion when she heard Rosa say, "...help...me."

Iris looked back over her shoulder, down at Rosa in her waning moments.

Iris wanted to aid her, but this was it, this was her opportunity to start over, to make her exodus from the streets, so Iris made a cross over her chest then wiped down the door handle and jetted.

For weeks rumors swirled. Home invasion. Revenge for some foul act. No one knew what really happened though. Only that a young couple had been killed in their prime. A mystery that would never be solved.

But one thing that certainly had no place in the rumor mill was Iris's engagement. It was real; Shamari had proposed and Iris had accepted.

The first couple days of wearing her ring, Iris thought of Capri. Imagined what life was going to be like without his influence. Wondered could they still be friendly, knowing he may never see the streets again. Secretly, she wanted that, but nowhere near as much as she craved normality.

213

"What are you smiling about?" asked Shamari.

Iris said, "I'm happy and free to live and be who I want to be."

NOW WHAT, RIGHT? Well...

For weeks rumors swirled. Home invasion. An inside job. A political cover up. Revenge for some foul act. There were in a couple activists suggesting assassination. The only place no doubt lied was cause of death.

A young New York couple in their prime shot to death, headlines had read.

Shandy Walton, his sexy PR, had taken hold of the nonprofit organization, something she had always planned on doing since the inception of ACCOUNTABILITY WHERE IT COUNTS. The rest of Stink's assets were frozen, pending investigation. And guess who'd been assigned the case? Bob Moore. He'd signed on as a special agent for the FBI.

While Capri was being lined up for a homicide conviction, and Stink was being memorialized online and on the streets, Iris was getting engaged. Shamari had asked Iris to marry him right after his team had handed Peyton Manning and the Colts one of his worse defeats.

Iris thought she was in love. The sex was great, the exclusiveness was different and down right good, and Shamari was acclomplished. So, she had accepted.

The first couple days of wearing her diamond clustered ring, having always been the side dish on Capri's plate, Iris couldn't believe someone really wanted to wife her.

Thoughts of her past were still looming though, a constant

recurrence. She imagined the future without her crew, and then seconds later, fantasized about the fast lifestyle in her rearview. She wondered could she still be friendly with Capri. Secretly, she wanted that, to be friends with her first love. At the same time, she wanted the normalcy that only Shamari had been able to provide. She would sometime simper when thinking of Christine. Word on the streets was Christine was loosing a lot of weight and sleep, and clocking hours at a local clothing store on 125th Street.

Guess Iris was the lucky one after all, huh?

Until the day she said, "I'm happy, and I'm free to live and to be who I want to be."

"It depends on one's definition of happiness and freedom to live," Shamari had replied, in just a wife beater and some untied tan construction Timberlands. Iris thought it was funny, even cute since she'd made a commitment to diet on just penis.

"Where are your pants?" she asked, shutting the front door to his stucco palace. She'd just returned from an early morning jog through his northern New Jersey neighborhood. She was breathing like a runner, one who'd just completed a marathon, in her spandex, Air Max and track jacket.

"I was waiting for you."

Iris went for a bottle of spring water in the nearby cooler, drank then said, "You want me like this? All sweaty? Legs all tight? I ran five miles this time, you know."

Shamari joined Iris in the kitchen, walking right into her words, into her periphery. "Yeah, I do want you. After I tell you something."

Iris drank a few more heaping gulps of her bottled water, then said, "Can I take a shower first?" Iris still couldn't believe her fiance wasn't wearing any bottoms, or that he was her fiance. "You can join me," she added, ogling him fervently.

This had come out rather easy, "I followed you!"

Iris grinned, "While I ran, huh?" No man had ever followed her who didn't just want a good time.

Shamari was close to her now, and she could smell the alcohol on his breath more as he whispered, "No, not while you ran, sweety." He kissed the side of her mouth, moved the sweat dampened hair siding her face behind her ear. She was a beautiful woman to him, one he could show off to his NFL buddies. Even with her shortcomings.

Shamari kissed her entire mouth with his second showing of affection real ruggedly. Normally that would turn Iris on; not this time though. It was discomforting, empty of passion.

"Are you drunk, Mari?" she asked, subtly lobbying for space.

"I followed you--"

"Where, Shamari? I didn't go anywhere else. I hardly go anywhere. The library, the grocery store, the spa. Where did you follow me to, and what did you see?"

"--to Stink's house... last month."

Iris took her backside off the countertop, sat her water bottle where her ass had just been. "You slurred something about Stink?" she quizzed.

"Yes, I did. I said, I followed you that day you left my bed. I followed you."

"What are you talking about?"

"You went inside; two days later I see on two different channels the owners of that house were found dead."

"Wha--? I don't know what you are talking about."

She could smell the liquor on his breath again. He was that

close.

"Yeah, you do, Iris. It was all over the news. And I followed you there."

Iris stammered, "They were... dead when I got there."

"So, why didn't you call the police?" asked Shamari with his face balled up.

Iris had no answer.

Shamari told Iris, "Just thought I'd let you know that!"

"They were... already dead."

"And you never speak of it to me, after laying up in my house for a month, accepting my proposal. Why didn't you come back here and tell me?!"

"I really don't know, but I didn't do it."

"Right!"

Shamari turned his back to Iris, started towards the spiraling staircase leading up to the second landing of his home. "So, again I say... it depends on one's definition of happiness and freedom to be who they want to be..."

AUTHOR'S NOTE

All right, alrigt--yeah, there will be another installment to the Street Generals Series! I've already started writing the next script. There's just too many dimensions to my character Iris. And now she has this pro football boyfriend with a dark side of his own. He has to have some sort of imbalance within, to let a month go by without mention of his suspicions, right? We're talking a double murder, not shoplifting.

Will they still wed? Will she relapse? And what about her first love? Murder was the case.

Thank you Meka for aiding and abedding me in this project. I love you, darling!

Made in the USA
Middletown, DE
07 May 2022